Born in Meknès, Morocco, in 1958, **Abdelilah Hamdouchi** is one of the first writers of police fiction in Arabic and a prolific, award-winning screenwriter of police thrillers. He is the author of *Whitefly* (2016) and *The Final Bet* (2016) and his novels have been translated into English, French, and other languages. He lives in Rabat, Morocco.

The Butcher of Casablanca follows *Bled Dry* (2017) as the second book in the Detective Hanash Crime Series.

Peter Daniel, a long-term resident of Egypt, has worked as a teacher of Arabic as a foreign language and an Arabic-to-English translator for many years.

D1008126

NO LONGER PROPERTY
SEATTLE PUBLIC LIBRARY

The Butcher of Casablanca

Abdelilah Hamdouchi

Translated by

Peter Daniel

hoopoe

AN IMPRINT OF AUC PRESS

First published in 2020 by
Hoopoe
113 Sharia Kasr el Aini, Cairo, Egypt
One Rockefeller Plaza, New York, NY 10020
www.hoopoefiction.com

Hoopoe is an imprint of the American University in Cairo Press
www.aucpress.com

Copyright © 2020 by Abdelilah Hamdouchi
Protected under the Berne Convention

English translation copyright © 2020 by Peter Daniel

All rights reserved. No part of this publication may be reproduced, stored in a
retrieval system, or transmitted in any form or by any means, electronic, mechanical, photocopying, recording, or otherwise, without the prior written permission of
the publisher.

Dar el Kutub No. 11979/19
ISBN 978 977 416 968 7

Dar el Kutub Cataloging-in-Publication Data

Hamdouchi, Abdelilah
        The Butcher of Casablanca / Abdelilah Hamdouchi.— Cairo: The
American University in Cairo Press, 2020.
        p. cm.
        ISBN 978 977 416 968 7
        1. English fiction
        2. English literature
        823

1 2 3 4 5   24 23 22 21 20

Designed by Adam el-Sehemy
Printed in the United States of America

1

HE HUMMED A FAVORITE TUNE as he went about his gruesome chore. When he was finished, he arranged the body parts in two garbage bags. Then he cleaned the floor, showered, and put on a change of clothes. He stretched out on the bed, lit a cigarette, and took a deep, delicious, triumphant puff. He had eliminated the thing that had been ruining his life and now all he had to do was to dispose of it.

His eyes darted back and forth apprehensively as the street narrowed to a cramped alleyway. He'd begun to imagine ghosts lurking in the darkness. He felt a surge of anger. He knew the source of his fear was the nauseating odor of decaying flesh assaulting his nostrils.

He jerked to a halt, extracted a cigarette from his pocket, and lifted the lighter to the tip, as if smoking would help him lug the bags. He changed his mind, picked up the bags, and lurched forward, wheezing heavily as he peered nervously into the dark recesses.

He had selected this spot after thorough research. It was in a calm, sparsely inhabited neighborhood far from where he lived. More importantly, there was a huge dumpster that never seemed to be completely full, unlike in other neighborhoods where the dumpsters quickly filled to overflowing and garbage bags were heaped around them.

He rolled the two bags into the bin, making sure they settled at the very bottom so they would be the last things the waste pickers ferreted through. As his fears evaporated, his face relaxed into an enigmatic smile. He cast a smug look around him, congratulating himself on how perfectly he had carried out his plan. There was no doubt about it. He was intoxicated with his victory.

Detective Hanash was in the garden with his German shepherd, Kreet—a "police dog," as the breed is called in Morocco—who could see through walls and whose thunderous bark caused young and old to jump in fear. Hanash unhooked the leash, leaving Kreet free to approach the bowl containing the chow Hanash prepared himself from leftovers mixed with chicken broth. The dog cast Hanash a grateful look, acknowledging his special effort, and attacked his food.

Naeema looked out from her bedroom window on the second floor and called down to her husband to hurry up and get ready. Her voice carried an extra dose of rebuke because she knew that if left to his own devices he would spend all day with his beloved Kreet. How he loved to play with that dog!

He never tired of watching him frolic, or of trying to keep up with the dog as he darted back and forth.

"That's enough now! Come in and get dressed," she cried impatiently.

She had laid out his favorite gray suit on the bed. It was just right for the pleasant weather. She'd spent a long time ironing his shirts, folding his clothes, and arranging everything in the suitcase. She was so excited, constantly muttering to herself, her eyes welling with tears of joy. How could she be otherwise? She had just received the news, in the early hours of the morning, that her daughter Atiqa had given birth to her second child—a son this time, as she'd hoped. Also, the delivery had gone smoothly with no need for a caesarean, unlike the first time.

This joyous news happened to coincide with a weekend, meaning they could travel up to Marrakesh to visit Atiqa. Naturally, Naeema would have preferred to be with her daughter during the delivery but it had occurred more than a week earlier than they had calculated. Not that this worried her, because Atiqa was surrounded by her husband's family and had the kindest care and attention.

Hanash was just as thrilled and eager to get on the road. He now had a grandson! He had to be frank with himself and acknowledge that he hadn't been very enthusiastic about visiting his daughter the last time, when she gave birth to a girl. He would never forget how overjoyed he was when his wife gave birth to their son, Tarek, after bearing two daughters. He

3

could not conceal how happy he was that his third child was a boy. It wasn't that he was averse to girls. He just felt that a father and son understood each other better. It was all about understanding, not about liking or disliking.

As he walked into the room, his wife shot him an appraising glance, put her hand to his forehead, and sighed. "You're all sweaty again!"

Naeema was desperate. She wanted to get on the road and out of the city as soon as possible. Hanash knew what she was thinking. She, like he and the rest of the family, feared that the telephone would ring at any moment, bearing the news of a crime and summoning Hanash to report to work immediately. Naeema had lost count of how many times this had happened. It happened when they tried to visit Atiqa after her first baby was born, and it happened during Naeema's last pregnancy, when he was called in to work just as she went into labor.

Manar, who shared her mother's fear, shouted, "I'm ready!" from the open door of her bedroom, and clapped her hands to encourage the others to get a move on.

"It's too early!" That was Tarek's grouchy voice coming from beneath his covers in his bedroom. "It's not even six yet. I haven't had to get up this early for ages."

Naeema opened the door to his room without knocking and responded with the irrefutable plea: "What if disaster strikes and your father gets called in to work? We'll never be able to leave." By "disaster" she meant a murder, of course.

"God forbid," Manar said. "As I said, I'm ready."

Tarek's room was a picture of anarchy. Clothes spilled from his open closet. An empty Coke bottle, a half-empty bag of potato chips, some French detective novels, and a jumble of papers were cluttered around his computer on his desk. His backpack, which should have been packed already, lay in a corner, empty. Naeema's eyes flashed as she took all this in.

"Is this the room of someone who plans to graduate from university and enroll in the police academy?" she cried in an exasperated voice. Tarek quickly sat up and smiled gently at his mother. Encompassing the room with a sweep of his hand, emulating his celebrated detective father, he said, "If you look carefully, Mom, you'll see method in this chaos. Think of it as a room where a crime occurred. You have to look at all these things as though they're clues."

His sister appeared beside his mother at his bedroom door and sneered down at him. She hated it when they spoke in police jargon at home. They'd nickname people after notorious criminals. Instead of saying, "I'm looking for something," they'd say, "I'm trailing the target." And rather than "I understood," it was "Ten-four!" or "Copy that." When they called out for their father, it was always "Hanash," his nickname from the force. And they called some of the neighbors "snitches." No one in this house ever said what they meant. They always left it to others to puzzle it out.

Hanash finished dressing, came out into the hallway, and barked his orders without looking at them, just as he did when ending a meeting at the department: "To your stations!"

They took up their positions in the car, which stood at the front door. Hanash reached for the ignition, then stopped and whispered in an affected way, "Damn! I almost forgot."

He got out of the car and rushed back into the house. Naeema's face tautened. She restrained herself from crying out in protest. If she got into a quarrel with him, it would only cause more delay.

From the back seat, Tarek said, "He didn't forget anything. He went back to change the hiding place of his gun. I bet he'll stuff it between the clothes in the dresser instead of locking it in the safe."

Manar shrugged indifferently. "He plans everything in bad faith."

Naeema swung around in her seat. "Don't speak about your father that way!"

"The defendant is guilty until proven innocent," Tarek put in mischievously.

Naeema quickly checked his wisecracking. "That was how it was in the Years of Lead. Today, with human rights, things are different. A person is innocent until proven guilty."

When she turned to face forward again, she saw her husband hastening toward the car. She breathed a sigh of relief and glanced down at her watch. "It's six thirty. We'll get to Marrakesh by ten." She smiled. "We'll be there in time to have breakfast with them."

Now in his fifties, Detective Hanash had only a few years left until retirement. Everything about him indicated that he had spent the greater part of his life interrogating thieves, forcing murderers to confess, and unraveling crimes. His real name was Mohamed Bineesa, but everyone called him Hanash—"the Snake"—because of how fast he could change his skin and strike.

Hanash would describe himself as a veteran from the generation of police officers whose careers spanned two eras. In Hanash's case, the "old era" was known as the "Years of Lead." It was the period when the Interior Ministry reigned supreme. The "Mother Ministry" they called it. It presided over a nadir for human rights. To go into a police station was to become "lost" and to come out was to be "reborn." Torture and abuse of power caused dozens of deaths per year. These were invariably chalked up to "suicide" or "natural causes." There were no checks or inquiries. Family members received the bodies of the "deceased" and buried them in silence without a word of protest. There were no legal avenues they could pursue, and should they attempt to file a complaint, events would take as nasty a turn as they had for the relatives they had just interred.

"The accused is guilty until torture proves him innocent," was the police motto in those grim days. Police stations were equipped with all the necessary instruments for the purpose. Some were primitive, such as the "falqa," or bastinado, whereby the soles of a victim's feet are raised, immobilized by binding the ankles to poles, and then subjected to repeated thrashing, leaving the victim unable to walk for days. Variants involved electric shocks or hanging the victim by his feet until the skin flayed. Then there was the horrifying "tayyara," the airplane—the technique of keeping a victim suspended until he eventually went mad.

There was a vast gulf between the "truth" in the depositions that illiterate suspects were forced to sign with a thumbprint and the actual crimes or delinquencies they allegedly committed. The literate, for their part, affixed their signatures in writing to fabricated confessions after varying degrees of physical and psychological coercion. Therefore, it would not be inaccurate to say that a significant portion of the prison population consisted of innocent people.

The judiciary in those days functioned by remote control, while dates of arrest were manipulated so that some detainees could enjoy police hospitality for endless months before seeing a courtroom.

Yet, there were people who hailed this situation as a great achievement and a service to society. It rid the country of criminals so you could roam the streets till dawn with no fear of harm. Repression in exchange for security: the ideal system for reducing crime rates. The criminal knows exactly what he risks before venturing to commit a crime: death under torture inflicted merely to force him to confess to stealing a wallet, or because he failed to pay a bribe when arrested as drunk and disorderly, or because he'd had the audacity to stand up to the police or even to attempt to flee. The most vicious criminal could be transformed into a police informant in exchange for simple services or payoffs after being let loose to engage in petty theft without causing physical harm or injury.

Given the state of public rights, it was sufficient, from a political standpoint, to be a "good citizen"—meaning never reading books or purchasing opposition newspapers, never tuning in to foreign radio channels, and being content with official news broadcasts, minding your own business and never sticking your nose into places it didn't belong, keeping all curiosity about what was happening in the world around you in check, never criticizing and only praising, always returning home early in the evening so as to avoid being picked up by a police patrol (with or without cause); in short, never doing anything that might bring you into contact with the police—in order to live safely and securely, and to die in peace.

Detective Hanash had spent about half his career in the "old era." He started out as a simple security guard, on his feet up to eighteen hours a day. Driven by poverty, deprivation, and an inferiority complex, he persevered until he was promoted to officer, inspector, and then detective. Over the course of twenty years he worked in all departments and was posted to several cities. It was in Tangiers, where he headed the crackdown on hashish smugglers, that he acquired both his wealth and his fame. It was an experience that he would always picture as a radiant monument emitting a golden gleam.

And now he lived in a villa in the center of Casablanca, a sturdy building from the colonial era when villas were grand, with high ceilings, spacious rooms, and balconies that over-looked lush gardens.

The transition to the "new era" was a permit to cross the threshold into the twentieth century. The reforms which were taken to absorb political tensions would subsequently fortify the state against the waves of havoc and devastation unleashed by that season known as the "Arab Spring." Virtually overnight, prisons disgorged their political detainees and millions of dirhams worth of compensation was paid out beneath the rubric of "equity and reconciliation." In a demonstration of its skill in waging revolution against itself, the Moroccan regime appointed as prime minister a former left-wing opposition leader who had been sentenced to death in absentia.

In a short time everything changed. "The plushest offices are now occupied by former political detainees" went a commonly told joke about the many who had moved from putrid cell to air-conditioned office.

The reforms precipitated a total metamorphosis in the country's political life, and an independent press burgeoned. But the greatest problem for the police in "new era" was that, at first, they didn't know how to function without the familiar tools. Police stations were ordered to remove all torture equipment and put up signs saying "The police are at your service." They now had to respect the limitations of provisional detention and free suspects without obtaining confessions or other information that had been won so easily with the usual methods. Generally (in the old era), suspects received their first beatings on their way to the police station, where they would be treated with slaps, kicks, and curses before being subjected to the falaqa, tayyara, electric shock, and other such treatment at the hands of the official torturers, after which they would confess to crimes they never committed or that they intended to commit in the future. Now, investigators had to interview suspects as though they were VIPs, write up depositions promptly, and exert immense effort to persuade suspects to sign them, which they might refuse merely because they didn't like the wording. Those influenced by American TV shows would even insist that they be read their rights and demand a lawyer.

With the end of the era of repression in exchange for security, the element of fear was gone and crime proliferated. The police insisted they were working as hard and dedicatedly as they could. But human rights meant they could not extract confessions by force and democracy meant they could not force an answer on a suspect.

It took some time and retraining before the situation improved. Meanwhile, the numbers of deaths due to torture in prison dwindled to almost zero and, moreover, some of the most notorious "executioners" were prosecuted. Undoubtedly, abuses still existed, but they were no longer systematic as was the case in the past.

Detective Hanash had experienced the transformation and had been part of it. He too had to change with the times.

In the "old era," especially when he was stationed in Tangiers and his work brought him in contact with hash-smuggling circles, he had raked in substantial sums. Now he only accepted gifts of high symbolic value. Moreover, ever since moving to Casablanca, his workload had doubled. It had also grown more difficult, now that all his old "executioner" friends had been put out to pasture.

The criminals of the "new era" were not only fearless, they were craftier. Armed with knowledge of police investigations and examination procedures, they destroyed evidence and laid false clues to lure police into an inextricable maze.

Hanash devised a system of his own to come to terms with the "new era." A major component was the dozens of confidential informants or "CIs": the snitches and squealers on whom he showered token rewards, in exchange for which information reached him faster than lightning. He had CIs in the media and cultural worlds, in all the notorious neighborhoods, in business and political circles, in bars, brothels, nightclubs, and even deserted areas. There was not a single unsolved case on Hanash's record, thanks to his network of spies that spanned all social strata.

Another element of his system was the excellent technique he had established for obtaining confessions through "soft torture," which left no marks as it relied primarily on psychological pressure that combined lures and threats, traps and tricks, wearying suspects to the point that they'd say whatever they were told to say.

Nor should we forget his detective's nose, which, like a sixth sense, enabled him to form an impression of a person the moment he met them and guided how he conducted his interrogations. Then, with an ear attuned to changes in the pitch of the suspect's voice and the rhythm of his or her breathing, he'd cull the truth from the verbal chaff. Finally, we must mention his trademark piercing investigator's glare that made you shiver and avert your eyes for fear of the torrent of accusations about to assail you.

Hanash was usually surrounded by people and rarely had time for himself. As soon as he woke, he'd find several urgent cases on his plate. He had to interrogate thieves and murderers, hear dozens of false confessions, shatter masks, and spend endless hours listening to lies told by suspects and witnesses. He also had to supervise his team, head out to crime scenes or to the morgue, and plow through reams of technical reports that, more often than not, had little useful substance for his work.

Five months ago, during a high-profile case in which a prostitute and her lover were found brutally murdered, one of his inspectors shot him at point-blank range in his office. Miraculously, he survived, but was in a coma for three days. He felt no pain, no comfort, no sense of whether he was alive or dead. But at one point, while he lay there on that hospital bed, immobile and attached to life by feeding tubes, he saw an angel standing at the foot of his bed saying, "God loves you, Hanash. That's why he sent someone to drive a bullet into your chest."

After he came to, those words stayed with him and, to his amazement, he saw his character undergo several changes. It was as though he truly were a snake changing its skin; as though he were a man who'd been living on some other planet and had come back to Earth. He saw his life pass before him: a train of lying, greed, betrayal, egotism, abuses. He shed streams of tears and realized there was another world out there. A purer world, even if being a policeman was a filthy job.

After a short period of recovery, Hanash returned to work, albeit slowly. One of the first things he did was to move out of the office where he was shot. He also changed his attitude toward his men. In the past he had viewed them with suspicion and vested absolute power in the officer he had chosen to spy on them, despite that officer's low rank. It was that same officer who shot him and who then took his own life in desperation when it was discovered he had stolen money from a crime scene. It goes without saying that, after the surgery, Hanash was incredibly feeble. He could not even urinate standing up. He no longer entertained pretty women like he had in the past. He even cut off his longstanding affair with dear Bushra, the village girl he'd met in Tangiers.

The car sped through the empty streets. There was no traffic at this early hour on Saturday, the first day of the weekend. The trip promised to be quick and pleasant. Naeema flicked through the radio channels in search of popular tunes suitable for a family occasion. She nodded rhythmically and hummed along to the music. Manar rested her head against the window and tried to sleep. Tarek cracked open a detective novel and began to read.

They were driving as fast as the law permitted in the city. Naeema was holding her breath until they passed the city limits and made it to the highway.

She sighed and said, "Oh, Atiqa, you're so far away in Marrakesh. If only you could live here. I could be by your side and help you bring up your children."

"Property is cheaper in Marrakesh than in Casablanca. Her husband was able to buy an apartment," Hanash said, his eyes on the road.

"They had to borrow," scoffed Manar, her eyes still closed.

Before Naeema could respond, she heard the sound she had dreaded. Hanash's phone rang once, twice, a third time. He exchanged nervous glances with his wife as he slowed the car.

"Who'd call me up at this time in the morning?"

Naeema mouthed a silent prayer.

Before she could beg him not to answer, he pressed "reply" and held the phone to his ear as he kept his eyes on the road. He listened attentively for a full minute, uttering only brief expressions of deference and respect as he pulled over to the side of the road. Finally, he bowed his head as though in the presence of the caller and said, "Yes, sir, I'm on my way to Marrakesh to congratulate my daughter on her newborn son. No, we haven't reached the highway yet. . . . Yes, sir. . . . Of course, sir."

Naeema felt a sharp spasm in her empty stomach. Manar and Tarek stiffened and stared glumly at their laps. They felt sorrier for their mother than they did about the cancellation of the trip. Tears had begun to spurt from Naeema's eyes even before her husband told them they had to turn back. She moaned. Her breathing grew labored. She was so angry she couldn't even look in his direction. She couldn't believe this was happening again—exactly as it had with Atiqa's first. She had thought that, for once, he would refuse to be called in, no matter what.

"That was his excellency the chief of police, himself, on the phone. They found the severed limbs of a mutilated corpse in a dumpster in Rue Juncor."

Naeema closed her eyes. She felt her daughter's hand on her shoulder. But what good was solidarity when it could alter nothing? She didn't have the power to make her husband say no to the chief of police.

"I have to get back," Hanash said sadly. "A dismembered mutilated body in a dumpster. This is something that doesn't happen in Casablanca every day."

He realized he was wasting his breath. No matter how he built up the horror of the crime, his wife would not sympathize. He'd never seen her this distressed.

She was crumpled in her seat, her eyelids pressed closed as though determined not to see the car return the same way it had come and as though she wanted to block out the voice of Manar, who was trying to console her: "I'll call up Atiqa right away to apologize and—"

Her father cut in. "Tell her we'll visit her as soon as possible. If I solve this homicide today we can start out again this evening."

"When has a murder ever been solved on the same day it was committed?" Naeema fumed without opening her eyes or moving her head.

Tarek, flicking back a lock of hair that had fallen over his forehead, said, "Of course, one purpose of the mutilation is to conceal the identity of the victim and throw investigators off the perp's scent."

Manar huffed angrily and said, "Stop talking crap! You guys make me sick."

Hanash tuned out everything and everyone around him.

In a few hours, the news of the murder would be all over the internet and tomorrow morning it would be splashed across the front pages of the printed press. Crime gets great publicity and dramatic coverage because the sensational lures readers. Facebook users and online newspapers pounce on everything graphic, gory, and grisly, and then exaggerate, embellish, and dramatize it in order to attract attention, increase the number of followers, or boost the chances of indemnity for the victim. A severed and mutilated body discovered on a Saturday morning makes for a plump piece of news to serve readers fresh for breakfast.

Hanash swerved into a shortcut that took them back home quicker. As he deposited his family at the front door, he cast his wife an apologetic glance. It occurred to him to pull her toward him and place a kiss of gratitude on her forehead. He looked at her beautiful embroidered dress and his heart filled with pity. She'd been so excited and had taken such pains to prepare herself, and now her joy had turned to grief.

Hanash's phone rang insistently. Naeema slammed the door of the villa and disappeared. Tarek gave his father a conspiratorial wink and Manar gave him a sad smile. Before he drove off, he heard a yelp and a whimper. That, he knew, was caused by a kick from his wife venting her fury on his most faithful friend. He checked a surge of anger. At times like this, he thought, marriage was a form of punishment for anyone who opted for a career with the police.

2

THE STREET THAT LED TO the crime scene was broad and almost empty. It was about seven a.m. There was no traffic and few pedestrians were out. He rounded the corner into a narrow street where the dumpster was located and entered the swarm of official vehicles of all sorts: police cars, Civil Protection Department vehicles, ambulances, cars belonging to the forensics technicians—the FTs, as they called them in the force. As he got out of his car he heard a voice from the crowd held back by the crime-scene tape saying, "There he is! Detective Hanash, the chief investigator."

His temples throbbed. It happened every time he encountered a homicide. He stopped a few feet away from the two plastic bags that contained the severed body parts and casually scanned the vicinity. It was one of his first steps when reaching a crime scene. He was like a filmmaker selecting the best angle to place the camera. It was his habit to proceed slowly and deliberately, sometimes infuriatingly so. To those unfamiliar with him, it gave the impression that he didn't know what he was doing, but actually he was giving rein to his detective instincts, hoping they would give him the first flash of inspiration to help him draw up his action plan.

His right-hand man, Inspector Hamid, came up and grumbled a greeting of sorts. He was especially grumpy-looking this morning. That was due less to the hideousness of this crime scene than to the fact that he had been torn from his bed while suffering a vicious hangover. He recited the steps that police and forensics had taken so far as though taking an oral exam.

Inspector Hamid lived alone in a small apartment not far from Hanash. He had lost his mother some months ago and her death came as much more of a shock than he would have imagined. She had suffered from Alzheimer's and he had looked after her by himself. He cooked for her, bathed her, treated her like a disabled child. He had put marriage out of mind as long as she was alive. But now that she had passed away and that burden had been lifted, he once again tended to his grooming and clothing. In his early thirties, he had a tall, erect, and athletic build. Sharp, perceptive eyes were set in a poker face with an enigmatic smile that never left his lips. He was Hanash's most trusted man.

Hanash could tell that Hamid was hung over and that he'd taken a cold shower and downed several cups of coffee just so he could keep his eyes open. Then he'd dressed so hastily that he hadn't buttoned his shirt properly. Not that there was anything wrong with that. Today was supposed to be a day off, after all.

Aware that his breath still smelled of last night's booze, Hamid addressed his boss from a distance. "I'm sorry you had to call off your trip, sir."

"I left Naeema at home in tears."

Hamid had become like a member of Hanash's family. After his mother's death, Naeema looked after him like an orphaned child. Eventually all formalities between him and Hanash's family vanished and he became an essential presence on all occasions, and even when there was no occasion at all.

"What do you have so far?" he asked Hamid as he continued to scan the area, taking in every detail.

"Female, adult, light complexion . . . um . . . age, weight, hair color, other features indeterminate."

"What are you saying?"

"Extreme violence, sir. The victim's been expertly cut up."

The forensic technicians had nearly finished their tasks of searching for anomalous marks, lifting fingerprints, and collecting any items that might offer a clue to the killer or killers. A forensics photographer was snapping pictures of the dumpsters and their surroundings. When he saw Detective Hanash approach, he halted his work, stood up, and nodded a greeting. The other technicians did likewise. Hanash muttered a greeting in return as he stepped toward the two bags and took a first look.

He grimaced in revulsion and jerked back, suppressing a violent desire to spill the nonexistent contents of his stomach.

"Those are just the lower limbs . . . minus the genitalia," spat out Hamid.

Hanash issued his first instructions of the day: "Search for the rest of the body parts. They may not be far away, in other bins."

Covering his nose with a handkerchief, he bent over the bags again. Hamid took a step forward and said, "We got the guy who called in this atrocity. He's over there."

He pointed toward a waste picker standing next to a policeman, who guarded him as though he might flee.

They were distracted by a sudden commotion. At first, Hanash thought they must have found the rest of the body. Instead, the assistant chief of police—the ACP—flanked by two smug-looking officials, appeared with a sour look on his face, as though peeved that no one had rushed forward to greet him. Pale, with deep-set eyes, he was in civilian clothes since it was a weekend. His two sidekicks looked more like businessmen than higher-ups in the law-enforcement hierarchy. Hanash came up, shook their hands respectfully, and said wryly, "Come this way, please."

He led the ACP to the first bag. Flies flew off it. The official's nose wrinkled as the nauseating stench assaulted him and forced him to stagger backward.

"We found two bags here. They contain only the lower limbs of the victim," Hanash informed him.

The ACP raised his voice to an authoritative growl to disguise his discomfort. "And the rest of the body? You haven't found it yet?"

"We've initiated a search in the nearby neighborhoods."

"Witnesses?"

Hanash thought the official both pretentious and premature. Nevertheless, he responded, "Nothing yet, sir."

"And the murder weapon? Have you found it yet?"

Hanash failed to suppress a scornful grunt. Talk about a dumb question, he thought. Did the ACP think the killer had slaughtered his victim and severed her limbs right here and then left behind his knife as a gift to the police to make their job easier?

Officer Hamid came to the detective's aid. Forcing his mouth into a deferential smile, he told the assistant chief: "We have the person who called in the homicide."

The ACP ignored the officer, as though he were too low to address. Still glowering at Hanash, he said with undisguised disdain, "Send the limbs to the medical examiner and keep me posted on the progress at every stage."

Hanash nodded curtly and turned away before the official swiveled to head back to his car, accompanied by his two companions.

Hanash gave Hamid a commiserating smile. That ACP was a pompous ass. Then he cast another look over the "crime scene"—metaphorically speaking, since the actual murder must have taken place elsewhere. The team from CPD—the Civil Protection Directorate—had taken custody of the plastic bags and were toting them to their vehicles. He had some brief conversations with a couple of field-evidence technicians, but didn't press for details because none would be available until after the autopsy and lab tests.

More immediately, he was eager to hear that they found the rest of the body. His first impression was that this homicide had been planned with great precision, that the perpetrator probably acted alone, and that he had cleverly eliminated his traces.

Hanash knew from experience that revenge was generally the motive behind such gruesome incidents and that the perp would not have the slightest doubt that his victim deserved this fate.

As he waited for one team of inspectors to return from their search of other dumpsters and for a second team to return from canvassing residents in the vicinity, he scanned the windows of the nearby apartment blocks. A number of heads ducked out of sight as though to escape his probing glare. He scowled in their direction as though they were accomplices. From his feel for the case so far, the perp wouldn't be from around here. He would have transported the bags by a vehicle of some sort from a remote location, following a carefully conceived and well-executed plan.

Hanash caught sight of Hamid speaking with one of the forensic technicians. He felt confident that Hamid was doing his job as professionally as always, despite a splitting headache from his Friday-night drinking session. Hamid left nothing to chance. He had an eye for details, refrained from drawing rash conclusions, and hated idle speculation.

The detective was not keen to question the waste picker. If the guy had anything to say, he would have already told

Hamid. Maybe he was pretending to know something important as a way to command some respect. No one from the sector of waste pickers, garbage grubbers, and dumpster divers had been promoted to CI yet, unlike parking attendants, street peddlers, shoe shiners, and some itinerant vendors. Waste pickers and their ilk were foul and dirty. They drove bicycle carts as they made the rounds of bins, poking through bags of garbage in search of the most trivial items that, to them, had some value, and tossing them into their carts to flog later in the junk market. For the sake of a few dirhams, waste pickers would claw through garbage bags, scatter trash and filth all over the place, and land street cleaners in trouble with residents.

To Hanash, the waste picker was barely a notch above a beggar. Despite this, he beckoned to the waste picker, who lurched toward him with his head bowed. Hanash took in the pockmarks in his dark complexion. But otherwise he seemed like a tall and sturdy young man. He could have been a construction worker or a porter and earned many times more than what he made from rummaging through refuse. But appearances can be deceptive. Perhaps he suffered from some incurable disease, Hanash thought as he inspected the young man's face more closely.

"You're the one who found the two bags, aren't you? What did you see?" Hanash asked.

The waste picker looked at him with the stunned gaze of someone who had just emerged from a horror film. He shook his head, unable to speak. Hanash gave him an encouraging nod, to no avail. So he commanded, "Open your mouth. Speak. What were you doing here?"

"I . . . I was just trying to make a living as usual." His body trembled, almost feverishly. "I open up bags to see if they have anything worth taking. Those two bags looked weird at first sight."

"Did you open them?"

The young man shuddered. But he nodded and continued as though accustomed to offering help. "I thought the first bag might contain an infant. I once saved a baby's life. I found him in a dumpster in a cardboard box. The cats would have torn into him if I hadn't gotten there in time. I called the police. They came and thanked me. Their chief even gave me a pack of cigarettes."

"I said, did you open the bag?"

"Well . . . yes and no, sir. It was already slightly open. I took a look. Then, when I reached inside . . ."

Tears streamed from his eyes. He gulped for air, staring at Hanash as though he had seen a ghost. He clamped his lower lip between his teeth and let out an agonized whimper.

Hanash gave the young man time to catch his breath.

"If only I hadn't," the man went on. "I felt soft human skin. I thought maybe it was an animal. But when I saw the toes . . . Oh, I wish I'd never seen that!"

"Did you see who put the bag in there?"

"No, sir."

Hanash fixed him with a stern, skeptical glare. "What time did you get here?"

The young man looked down at his watch and answered confidently, "At a quarter to six."

"Now, think carefully. Did you see anybody here or in the vicinity, even in one of the streets nearby?"

The young man spoke nervously, caught off guard by the question. "If this weren't a Saturday, there would have been some activity around that time. People on their way to work . . . But this being a Saturday, people were sleeping in. So . . . no, sir, I didn't see anyone. The streets were completely empty. Whoever put those bags in there must have done it sometime in the middle of the night."

Hanash eyed him suspiciously. "How do you know that?" he asked and scrutinized the young man's face as he answered.

"It's my job, sir. I can tell each of the residents here from their garbage. I'm absolutely sure that the man who did this is not from this part of town."

Hanash's eyes widened in surprise. He thought about holding on to this young waste picker for a bit, perhaps even adding him to his list of CIs. Maybe he knew more than he let on.

Their eyes met and Hanash flashed him a smile. The waste picker quickly averted his gaze. Hanash decided to leave the question as to whether to bring in CIs until later. He didn't have enough to go on yet, and in general, homicides such as this are crimes of passion. They're committed for personal reasons, often by people with no criminal record who had been living calm, ordinary, and respectable lives until something made them snap. He recalled the last case of this sort. The horror of it had stunned the entire country and pre-occupied newspapers and social-networking sites for weeks. It involved a simple quarrel between the owner of a popular kofta restaurant and a neighbor who grew so fed up with the smoke from the grill that he began to blackmail the restaurant owner. One night, the latter lured the neighbor into the restaurant, stabbed him, chopped him up, and sold his flesh mixed into the ground beef.

At last the search team returned, weary and dirty, failure written on their faces. Hamid went up to Hanash and shook his head sadly. "Negative on the dumpsters in this vicinity. I instructed another team to broaden the search and to coordinate with other teams, even if they have to cover the whole city."

Hanash nodded sympathetically. Then he curled his lip as he cast a last critical look around him. This wasn't where the murder was committed, after all. The crime scene was elsewhere. The body was only dumped here. Why this place, exactly? Where did he dispose of the upper portion of the body? You can't ID a victim without a face or hands to get prints from.

As he turned toward his car, he jerked his head at the waste picker and instructed the policeman guarding him, "Take him to the station, run an ID check, and take his statement."

3

CASABLANCA, THE CONSUMMATE CITY OF contradictions. Natives call it "the Ghoul" because of its power to frighten all newcomers and because it contains all the worst of under-developed capitalist societies. Though a city of high finance, big business, astounding economic growth, and rapid urban expansion, one is left mouth agape at how its elegant upscale neighborhoods, with their luxurious villas, nightclubs, and posh shopping centers displaying international brand names, stand cheek by jowl with overcrowded slums consisting of crudely made houses without proper sanitation facilities. It is those miserable hovels that supply the city with its many types of sellers of love, from the young beauties who staff the nightclubs to the old flaccid wretches who specialize in oral sex in doorways and dark alleys. From there, too, come the overworked factory girls for the industrial zone, not to mention the panoply of delinquents, religious extremists, and professional criminals.

*

Hanash parked his car and entered the police headquarters, located in central Casablanca. Actually, they were only a couple of kilometers from where the half a corpse was found.

Back in the Years of Lead, police stations (apart from the offices of the higher-ups) were almost as dismal and depressing for the staff as they were for inmates. And the Commissariat of Police was no exception. Corridors were dark and dank. The dilapidated offices had ramshackle desks, often without chairs. Files and folders were stuffed into cabinets without doors. Inspectors wrote their reports on antiquated typewriters that clicked and clacked as loudly as railway carriages. Light bulbs were either missing or layers of dust inhibited all but the feeblest light. Sinks were a rare commodity and those that did exist were generally out of order or dripped incessantly. Given the abysmal state of facilities in general, there was no need to speak of the toilets or the detention wards, let alone the torture chambers.

Before Hamash reached his office, his phone rang. When he saw the number, he decided it would be wiser to wait until he was alone. It was his wife. He really didn't have time for this right now. At first he was going to ignore the call, but he changed his mind when he recalled her anguish.

As he settled into his plush leather chair behind his desk, he summoned the will to call her back and speak gently regardless of how irately she spoke.

Her voice was filled with pleading. "Is there any hope we can still go?"

He fought back a surge of anger. He too would have preferred to be on the way to their daughter in Marrakesh. How he longed to see his grandson, hold him in his arms, and coo at him. Struggling to keep his voice under control, he said, "If only you knew, Naeema. I have a mountain of work. There was this horrific murder. We found half the body of a woman tossed in the garbage. Can you imagine? We still haven't found the second and most important half."

He didn't usually give his wife such information so early on in a case. But if he could spark her curiosity he might divert her from the subject of the trip. Normally she would have leaped at this piece of news and begun to shower him with questions, formulate hypotheses, and pester him for more information. The world of crime had become a part of her world. She had acquired a passion for the details, following investigations and devising theories. She had picked up so much of his inspectorial style that in the neighborhood she was nicknamed "the Viper," the wife of "the Snake."

But not today. She was on to his ruse.

"I don't want to hear about your work," she snapped.

"You're no longer interested in the latest crime?" He checked all hint of sarcasm in his voice.

"The crimes you inflict on me are quite enough!"

Hanash scowled. He picked up his office phone and punched a number. "Miqla, come to my office right away." Slamming down the receiver, he resumed the conversation with his wife. He spoke as gently as he could. "I appreciate the pain you feel, but—"

Suddenly she could no longer contain herself. All the pent-up resentment erupted in a torrent as she fought back her tears. "You only appreciate your work. You've always let me down. You've never been there when it really counted. You always leave me to cope on my own. My life with you has been nothing but hardship, misfortune, and disappointment. I wish I'd never married you. I wish I'd never even met you. What a rotten fate! A woman who marries a policeman knows nothing but hell. She'll never see a happy day in her life!"

Hanash remained calm and silent. He didn't try to cut her off and snarl at her as he usually did when he disapproved of what she was saying. This time he sympathized. He bowed into the storm and let it run its course, fighting any urge to interrupt her. He was sure that if he said anything at all, he would cause a breakdown. As she continued, she began to ramble and her voice grew vague as though she were speaking more to herself than to him. Eventually she managed to calm herself down and utter some words of apology.

The office phone rang. He ended the call with his wife and picked up the receiver of the office phone, looked at the number of the caller, let a few seconds pass, and then said gruffly, "What have you got?"

Officer Hamid's voice was filled with regret. "Canvassing led nowhere. No one in the vicinity heard or saw a thing."

"And the upper half?"

"The search is still in progress."

"Continue the search and keep me posted on every bit of information you get."

As soon as he hung up, he heard a knock on the door. Officer Miqla entered with an awkward greeting. Hanash's eyes narrowed in a long and lethal appraisal. Miqla was short and fat, with a small black mole protruding from the side of his nose. His suit was ridiculous, as drab and shapeless as a pair of pajamas.

Hanash snorted. "Did you roll out of bed and into the station? Didn't you take a look in the mirror? Are you sure you're even awake?"

The officer gave an unusually bold shrug. "This is the third time I've been deprived of my weekend, sir."

"Yes, I know," Hanash sneered. "And you'll be deprived of it a fourth time, a fifth time, and so on to eternity." He flashed a smile to let Miqla know that he'd only been feigning anger. He signaled the officer to a chair and assumed a sympathetic tone. "No one gets any rest in this job until they're dead and buried. Meanwhile, I want you to compile a list of all the open files of adult females reported as missing in the greater Casablanca area."

"Is there a picture of the victim or any identifying features?"

"Negative. As soon as I learn the tiniest detail I'll let you know."

Miqla performed a clumsy salute and shuffled out of the room. Hanash smiled to himself as he became absorbed in his own thoughts. He had to consider all possible angles. First, he wanted to identify the motive behind this murder. Evil pervaded the very marrow of this case. The perpetrator would have his own pathological rationale. Undoubtedly he thought he had a right to kill, took pleasure in the act, and reaped an emotional release from it. He would have taken great relish in mutilating and dismembering the body and savagely brutalizing the genitalia. Now he must be congratulating himself on his work. He was probably preparing a large breakfast for himself as he exulted in his triumph and the trouble and work he'd created for the police on the morning of the first day of their weekend.

Hanash glanced down at his watch, got up quickly, and left his office.

As he entered the Ibn Rushd University Hospital, which now had a new wing dedicated to the forensic sciences, Hanash recalled his friend Dr. Wahli, who had emigrated to Canada after despairing at the unimproved conditions of his profession at home. It was not until recently that there was direct contact between the chief medical examiner's office and the criminal investigations unit. In fact, strictly speaking, there hadn't been a forensics department until now. A group of doctors had been assembled to fill a gap for the past few decades, but that was it.

Despite improvements in this field (such as this new wing), there was still a lack of infrastructure and system. Every doctor had his or her own way of performing an autopsy, depending on their specialization—that is, if a court decided to bring in a doctor for an autopsy or a medical opinion to begin with. The prevalent view was that forensics was only about corpses or identifying kinship by DNA analysis, and that was it. Still, it was an improvement over the Years of Lead, when this field had a nasty reputation: the purpose of medical examiners was to serve the powers that be, to provide evidence to justify police actions, and to forge medical reports to cover up the torture and murder of people in custody.

Dr. Wahli's replacement was a graduate in forensics from one of the leading French universities in this discipline. Currently, she was also a professor at the Casablanca Faculty of Law, and devoted more time to teaching than she did to her work at the morgue. She refused to go out to a crime scene and, instead, delegated one of her trainees. She introduced herself officiously in rapid-fire French: "Dr. Wafa Amrani, chief of forensics."

This was the third time she had spoken with Hanash, yet she acted as though she didn't know him and his position in the police.

"Hello, professor. How are you doing? Even you have had to change your weekend plans because of this atrocity. Those limbs are all we found. We're still searching for the rest."

She conducted him directly into the autopsy theater. With its gleaming white-tiled walls, the room resembled a miniature mausoleum. The autopsy table was clean and shiny but exuded a peculiar odor. The medical examiner whisked the sheet off the half-corpse with a flourish as though she wanted to impress Hanash. She then extracted a small notepad from her pocket and recited her initial findings, indifferent to Hanash's grimace of disgust.

"Your victim is probably in her early twenties. Full-figured. Judging by the length of her legs she can't be more than five and a half feet tall."

She spoke confidently and matter-of-factly, without looking at Hanash, who she knew was holding his breath and attempting to look composed.

Trying to hide his discomfort at the pair of legs laid out before him, Hanash said, without budging from his place: "Are there no distinguishing features on those parts of the body?"

"Only rarely do the lower limbs, in themselves, serve to identify a person," the professor responded as though delivering a press statement. "Human feet and legs are very much alike, which makes it difficult to establish identity on the basis of them alone. In this case, the difficulty is compounded by the disfigurations that were inflicted postmortem on these limbs and the genitalia."

Hanash frowned as he struggled not to shift his eyes away from the table. "Maybe the excision of the reproductive organs was to hide a rape," he said. "Or perhaps it was to exact extra vengeance."

The medical examiner nodded, and added, "Whoever committed this atrocity is thoroughly cold-blooded. I find it hard to rank him among the human race."

Hanash suddenly felt very weary. "Could the victim be a prostitute? Or maybe a homeless woman?"

Dr. Amrani came around to the other side of the autopsy table and spoke as though the question didn't even merit a response. "There's nothing to suggest that."

She pulled the sheet back over the limbs and preceded Hanash toward the exit.

"I'll send you all my findings in an itemized report. But I can't promise you much until you find the other half."

As he was about to insert his key into the office door, he caught sight of a lone figure slouched on a bench a little farther down the corridor. It was the waste picker.

"Hey, you!"

The waste picker shot to his feet.

Signaling to him to stay put, Hanash asked, "Hasn't an officer taken down your statement yet?"

"No, sir."

"Stay there."

Entering his office, the detective flicked through his list of informants. But he had no reason to call any of them. He had nothing useful to give them yet. Not a shred of evidence or a fragment of a clue.

He was annoyed by the silence and lack of activity in the department on that weekend day. The FTs must be analyzing the paltry items that came their way. He glanced at his watch. It was getting on to one p.m. and he still had nothing to sink his teeth into.

He thought about phoning Hamid to check on the progress of the search for the rest of the corpse, but changed his mind. If they'd found anything, he'd be the first to know.

After a moment, he picked up his cell phone and dialed his home phone. His wife picked up immediately as though expecting his call.

"Are we going to go? Have you finished your work?"

He spoke slowly, trying to convey additional layers of meaning through the tone of his voice.

"I told you, it's impossible for me to leave. I'm up to my ears in work. I'll call up Atiqa and apologize to her and her husband. But if you want to go to Marrakesh together with Manar and Tarek, feel free."

Naeema hid her disappointment beneath a long sigh. He felt that she understood his situation.

Without a hint of reproach, she said, "You still haven't found a lead?"

Hanash smiled. He shifted some documents and relaxed back into his chair.

"We haven't found a thing yet. Nothing that can shed a bit of light on this case."

Naeema sighed again. Hanash sensed that she had lost her customary curiosity that would prod her to ask more questions.

"May God help you succeed," she said.

"It's best that the three of you go to Marrakesh without me," Hanash said despondently. "This case could drag on. We have a mutilated corpse and only the bottom half of it so far. We're still looking for the rest. I'd expected to have made some progress by now."

Naeema paused. She was about to remind him that this was exactly what had happened when their daughter gave birth to her first child and that he always broke his promise on important family occasions. However, she held back. Her husband's suggestion was an acceptable compromise.

"I'll give Atiqa your love and kisses and tell her how sorry you are you couldn't make it."

Content that he had resolved that problem, Hanash replaced the receiver and pressed the bell to call the guard at the door. The door didn't open. "Oh, it's the weekend," he muttered. He pushed himself out of his chair, walked over to the door, and opened it himself. He instructed the waste picker, who had been waiting in the corridor, to come into his office and close the door behind him.

Something about him bothered the detective. He seemed like a strong youth, but at the same time he looked tired and his eyes kept darting away. He'd have to get to the bottom of that.

Hanash asked him for his ID card. He took it, flipped it over, set it on the desk in front of him, and slowly turned his gaze back to the waste picker.

"So, Allal, the place where you found the bags, do you know it well?"

"Yes, I know it very well. I always go there at the same time so I can get to the garbage before the others."

Hanash looked at him closely. "So you were the first to find the bags. What time was that?"

Allal didn't hesitate for a second. "At a quarter to six."

"How do you know that none of your . . . colleagues got there before you?"

The young man smiled. "When you talk to the police you gotta tell the truth. And the truth is that the doormen at those buildings don't take the garbage out to the dumpsters before ten in the evening. By that time, the nighttime waste pickers are done for the day. I'm the first to get there in the morning before the garbage trucks arrive, which is at eight."

"Do you look through the garbage with your bare hands?"

"I use rubber gloves as a precaution. Garbage these days is not as clean as it used to be."

Hanash laughed. "When was garbage ever clean?" He contemplated the young man more closely. "You junkmen get around. Wherever there are garbage cans, you go there. I bet you got some junkman friends. I want you to help us. Get in touch with them and ask them about the rest of the body. Scratch my back, I'll scratch yours. You smoke?"

Allal stiffened as he tried to grasp the deeper significance of that question.

Hanash turned to a cabinet where he kept confiscated goods, opened it slightly so as not to reveal the contents, took out a pack of Marlboros, and tossed it to the waste picker.

"If you don't smoke, sell them."

He told Allal to go back outside and wait until an officer came to take down his statement. Allal said that he was ready to be of help whenever needed and ambled out of the room as though he had all the time in the world.

Hanash left the office dejectedly and headed to the nearby coffeehouse to have a bite to eat. He hadn't even had the chance to drink a coffee yet. None of the information he had would be of any use without a head and hands.

The search crews had returned empty-handed again. No trace of the torso. He'd convened a meeting of his staff to discuss an action plan, and now he felt the frustration build up inside him as he cast about for words. He fidgeted in his seat, irritated at the expectant looks of his officers. He was afraid a torrent of rebuke would escape his lips, as though they were somehow to blame, whereas they'd done the best they could. They were dog-tired after having spent hours rummaging through garbage and filth and inhaling all those putrid odors. Finally, he marshaled a cool head and forced his brow to relax. He smiled as he looked at each of his men, nodding his approval at their efforts.

"As you know, the first hours are of critical importance in the process of solving any crime. At the very least they help in formulating a workable hypothesis and staking out a trail that could lead to the perp or perps." He paused and took a deep breath. "Unfortunately, we have nothing so far. As you know, this is no ordinary homicide. The body's been dismembered and we still have only the lower limbs." He raised his voice. "Where's the torso? More importantly, where's the head? Where are the hands that will give us the fingerprints?"

Looking at each of his men in turn, he said, "Come on, speak. Say something. I want to hear what you have to say."

The officers fixed their gazes in midair, making them seem rather obtuse. None of them wanted to speak because they had nothing to show for their efforts. Also, if one of them ventured a stupid observation, Hanash might lash out at the offender with his venomous sarcasm and turn him into a laughingstock in front of the others. They were wary of that aggressive side of the Snake. Yet they also knew that one of them had to say something. Inspector Hamid nodded encouragingly at Officer Miqla, who was holding a file. He was the only one who had anything approaching a solid piece of information. Miqla cleared his throat. The file shook in his hands. He began to recite the information it contained without opening it, as though he had committed it to heart. He spoke in a mumble, pausing frequently to clear his throat.

"According to the available information in our database and all other law enforcement platforms, there is no missing-persons report filed for an adult female matching the attributes of the victim."

Hanash lurched forward in his chair and fixed Miqla with a glare. "What attributes do you have that make you think that you can use the word *attributes*?" he snarled.

Hamid quickly stepped in to smooth over the CO's outburst. He was the only one the Snake wouldn't bite. Shifting his eyes from one person to the next as he spoke, he said, "The perp or perps disposed of all the personal belongings of his victim. There are no identifying documents, no articles of clothing . . . zilch. Also—"

Hanash cut in abruptly: "Which means that without torso, hands, and head, we're going to be left sitting here, twiddling our thumbs."

He got up and strode across the room, swept aside the heavy curtain, flung open the window as far as possible, and looked out at the calm and almost empty street. The whole of Casablanca wished that every day of the week could be a weekend so they could always enjoy this tranquility. He took a deep breath. He needed to reconcile himself to the lack of progress while remaining open to all possibilities. He desperately needed all his men.

He turned to them again and smiled, looking at each of them in turn. "I know our hands are tied without a solid lead. Still, if we can't say anything yet about the victim, what can we say about her killer?"

The brief speech, given without a hint of reproach, made the men's face brighten with fresh enthusiasm. Now they were all keen to speak.

Inspector Bu'u said, "In my opinion, the killer probably acted on his own. He murdered his victim in his house, then packed her lower half in the trunk of his car and got rid of it at the dumpster where we found it."

Inspector Kinko's voice cut in with its chronic asthmatic wheeze: "Where did he dispose of the important part of the victim's body?"

"How do we know he disposed of it anywhere?" asked a corpulent officer, who thought himself astute. "This perp is very dangerous. He knows exactly how we work. He kept everything that might enable us to identify the victim: the face with its features, the hands with their fingers from which we could take prints."

In such meetings, as a rule, Hamid didn't intervene until after learning everyone's opinion. This time, however, he cut in: "The murderer's aim is to destroy all clues leading to the identity of the victim. He's operating on the premise that by concealing the identity of the victim he is forcing us to contend with the theory 'no body, no crime.'"

"We've got half a body," Hanash cautioned wryly. He leaned over his desk to pick up a small stack of photos of that half and distributed them listlessly, as though performing a futile exercise. The photos said nothing.

Hamid put in, in part to pick up his boss's spirits: "We'll assign as many men as available to combing every quarter of this city. We'll search every nook and cranny, under every stone if we have to. We've already notified every precinct and security agency in the city and in other provinces with instructions to contact us immediately in the event any body parts surface."

The officers, crime scene and autopsy photos in hand, began to speculate excitedly. Hanash settled back in his chair, closed his eyes, and let the words drift around him. He was tired and depressed. In all previous cases, he'd been able to discover a thread, however thin, and that thread would lead him to others that were thicker and surer. But this case was different. It was a whole project that been studied, planned, prepared, and carried out by an author who was familiar with police methods and how to elude them.

The others in the room could read what was going through the CO's mind from his grim expression, disinterest, and silence. They stopped jabbering and the room fell silent. Hanash sat up in his chair and fixed them with an intense gaze.

"What if the killer cut up the upper half of the body into little bits, smashed the skull, ripped the face apart, amputated the fingers, and then scattered all those bits and pieces into different streams, sewers, and canals? After all, his aim is to erase the identity of the victim."

Officer Hamid put in gloomily, "Or he might also be keeping the head at home, in his fridge. Who knows?"

45

*

That night, Allal went about his work with extraordinary enthusiasm. He called Hanash several times up to the early morning hours to "report," as though he were now an official employee of the state. Hanash constantly had to wake up his officers and dispatch them to the dumpsters the waste picker had indicated. Each time, they found themselves examining chicken carcasses, the remains of rotten sausages, or animal intestines.

In the month that passed since the half-corpse was discovered, Hanash grew increasingly grumpy. He couldn't bear to be among his aides, unable to express his satisfaction at any initiatives they took. Nor could he bear to talk about work with his wife or anyone else at home. Often unable to sleep, he'd get out of bed, put Kreet on a leash, and take long nighttime strolls to the place they had found the body or to other neighborhoods in the vicinity.

Naeema felt exasperated and at a loss. She sensed that Hanash had taken on too much and was unable to let time take care of things. She watched her husband grow tenser and more defeated by the day. He'd grown accustomed to solving crimes in record time and to receiving congratulations from his superiors and looks of admiration and esteem from friends and colleagues. But this case had severely shaken his self-confidence. And the press didn't help. He was deeply offended by the headline that mocked the "old snake who could no longer change its skin."

46

She did her best to comfort him and to encourage him to be patient. She'd remind him of his past achievements in the hope that this would gird him against giving in to despair and inspire him to muster his self-confidence, go on with his work, and prove his worth. But no matter what she said or did, he would turn away from her and sink deeper into his depression.

4

THE TELEPHONE WOULDN'T LET HIM finish shaving. He stood
in front of the bathroom mirror and a sink filled with bristles
and shaving foam. He'd only managed to shave the right
half of his face. Naeema stood at the bathroom door holding
his cell phone.

"It's been ringing nonstop," she said.

She waited as her husband slowly stroked the shaved half
of his face. He no longer seemed to care whether his phone
would bring him good news about his main case. He'd also
lost interest in the details of his other cases, which he had
mostly delegated to Hamid.

At last, he reached for the phone and put it to his ear. He
grimaced as though what he heard gave him heartburn. He
plopped his razor into the sink, wiped the remaining soap off
his half-shaved chin, and pushed past his wife to avoid speaking with her. His face was livid.

It was so crowded that it was hard to discern the police from
the civilians. Hanash's eyes came to rest on the large plastic

garbage bag. He avoided Hamid at first and he felt an urge to shout at the crowd of onlookers gawking from the other side of the crime-scene tape. Some journalists pushed forward, but the guards held them back and, at a gruff command from Hanash, forbade them from taking pictures. They grumbled and snapped some shots from a distance.

There were more techs from forensics this time. A few of them climbed into spacesuit-like overalls that made them look like astronauts and covered their faces with heavy masks. One of them plunged into the dumpster and began to poke at and sift through the bags and boxes. Another followed a specially trained police dog on a leash. A third fired his camera incessantly at everything from all angles.

Hamid approached and spoke in a hushed, strained voice. "It's the lower half of an adult female, again."

Hanash ignored him. He'd already learned most of the important details over the phone on the way over. He headed directly to the bag and cast a quick look inside. Grimacing in revulsion, he turned angrily in the direction of a member of the forensics team, who began to speak in an apologetic voice.

"The lower limbs and pelvis of an adult female. The thighs were mutilated by a sharp instrument."

Hamid, reading Hanash's mood, hurried over and said in a voice meant to soothe his CO's anger. "Miqla, Bu'u, and Baba are canvassing the nearby apartment blocks, shops, and stores. More than ten men are searching for the rest of the victim."

Hanash's blood boiled as he surveyed the scene. It was almost the same place as the last time. Only a couple of narrow streets away.

Hanash opened his mouth and snapped it shut again. He had nothing to say. He strode away from the bag containing the remains and then turned slowly in place, ignoring the wave of a journalist from behind the crime-scene tape. A number of thoughts passed through his mind, but he was only able to focus on one: This murder must have been committed by the same guy as the first.

Hamid noticed his boss's half-shaved face. Hanash preempted him. "I know," he said in a weary voice as he rubbed his hand over the stubble.

He scanned the area again and then yelled a command to his men: "Broaden the search for the rest of the body as far as possible. Spread out in all directions."

The detective didn't have to wait long this time. Only two streets away, a police dog sniffed out another bag next to a dumpster. It had been clawed open, exposing human remains. Police guards rushed over to the place and cordoned it off with crime-scene tape. Hanash's team hastened over, followed by a crowd of gawkers and journalists.

The disappointment came like a punch in the stomach. It was a mutilated adult female torso from which the head and fingers had been severed.

Hanash staggered backward and almost tripped. He erupted into a roar aimed at everyone around him: "Look for the head everywhere! Search the whole damn city, day and night!"

He suddenly thought of Allal. Where was that waste picker when you needed him?

Back in their labs, the forensic technicians pored over the items that had been culled from the crime scene, which, of course, were not plentiful. After conducting analyses and documenting their observations, they concluded that the perpetrator had covered his tracks very well. He left no fingerprints because he wore gloves. The garbage bags containing the remains had no brand name or logo. The second victim had been dismembered in the same manner as the first. Anything that might give a clue as to the second victim's identity had been systematically eliminated or mutilated beyond recognition. The information confirmed the detective's hypothesis that it was the same perp.

Professor Amrani not only submitted a timely report, but she invited Hanash to her office this time in order to spare him the discomfort of the autopsy theater. There was nothing of note to show him there, anyway. Just the horrid sight of mutilated human body parts.

Sensing Hanash's frustration, she knitted her brow and shook her head in dismay. There was not a hint of the professional sparkle in her eyes as she reiterated her findings.

"The second victim was subjected to even more extensive mutilation than the first. The motive could have been revenge. That likelihood is inescapable given the brutality with which the body was dismembered, marred, and mutilated. In this case, the murderer inflicted numerous slashes on the thighs and buttocks using a very sharp instrument, most likely a razor blade. This signifies that for him it was not enough just to kill the victim. He vented his rage against her after killing her." She paused, offered Hanash a commiserating smile, and said, "But none of this amounts to much without the head of the victim and the identifying features of the face."

"And the fingers, from which we could get her prints," Hanash added with a sigh. His shoulders slumped, as though he knew in advance that his next question was futile. "Is there any way we could learn something about the nature of the murderer's profession from the way he dismembered the two victims?"

"The limbs were severed more skillfully in the second case. The killer might be a butcher. But he is certainly not a surgeon."

Hanash smiled feebly as he extracted his ringing phone from his pocket and pressed "answer."

The chief of police's meeting with the Criminal Investigations Unit was restricted to senior officers and above. They jumped when he thumped a pile of newspaper articles and printouts from the online press on the desk. Gesturing toward them, he said frostily, "They're all about us. They're calling us negligent and incompetent. They're turning public opinion against us."

He snatched up a handful of articles and distributed them at random. Then he went over to a small table in the corner on which there were some bottles of mineral water. He poured himself a glassful and gulped it down in one go. Mohamed Alami, the chief of police, was the type of person whose every feature and gesture bespoke their profession. One would never doubt for a moment that he was a senior security official. His features were sharp, his expression stern. His every gesture projected authority and a readiness to use it. Even the way he spoke was awe-inspiring. It blended an element of courteousness with a firmness that left no room for a second's hesitation in carrying out his orders. He scrutinized his small audience briefly, then gestured toward the large map of Casablanca that stretched the full length of the wall. He indicated two large circles connected by a red line. There was no need for him to explain that those were the locations where the body parts of the two victims were discovered. He drew in a deep breath and addressed the men in a voice that carried a strong hint of ridicule.

"Let's have each of you read out the headline of the article you have in your hands."

They smiled awkwardly.

Alami looked straight at Hanash. "We'll start with you."

The detective recited his headline in a stiff but weary voice: "A new headless victim."

Inspector Hamid came next. He affected the deep, reverberant voice of a newscaster: "Casablancans alarmed by rumors of a serial killer who attacks women and mutilates their bodies."

The other headlines were equally sensational. Some invented lurid tales of other bodies discovered in other parts of the city. Others, probably inspired by Hollywood serial-killer thrillers, warned of a "Psychopath on a vengeance spree against women." Still others spoke of a "Killer on a rampage!" undeterred by a "negligent police force that was only spurred into action by bribes and extortion payments."

Commander Alami broke in with an uncharacteristic bellow: "Did you listen to all of that? The press hates us and they're turning public opinion against us. They're spreading panic in the city! They're inflating the number of murders. They're publishing sensationalist photos that have nothing to do with the victims. They're jacking up their sales at our expense!"

He paused briefly and resumed ruefully, "The times are gone when they feared our wrath. This is the age of the internet, freedom of the press, online newspapers, YouTube, and Facebook. Our Public Information Department has released statements denying all those rumors, but no one believes them." He'd begun to pace back and forth. "Some journalists are linking these crimes with terrorism and religious extremism!"

The chief let this remark hang in the air for a second. Hanash seized the opportunity to raise his hand and request to speak. After all, he was the main object of this discourse as long as he was the person in charge of the investigation, in his capacity as head of criminal investigations. His was the name most frequently mentioned in the press in connection with these crimes. He passed his tongue over his parched lips and struggled to dispel the blackness descending in front of his eyes.

"Those articles calling us negligent mean nothing," Hanash said. "All teams are working around the clock on this case. If we haven't made any progress on it so far, it's because these homicides are unique. We're looking at a pro, a guy who effaces the identifying features of his victims brutally yet systematically, leaving us without a trace to follow. He wants his crimes to be perfect but, as history has shown, there is no such thing as a perfect crime. Still, this killer is clever. He knows our methods so he uses sleight of hand. Is he a psychopath? Is he really out to avenge himself against women? Does he kill because he relishes the act? I should add that, apart from the MO, we have no concrete proof that the same murderer committed both homicides."

Snatching up several articles and brandishing them in front of Hanash, Alami interrupted him brusquely. "The reports that are submitted to me, and that I in turn submit to central headquarters, contain nothing. They offer no hope that the killer will be found, regardless of whether or not it is the same person."

"The fact that we've been unable to find the heads of the victims and that there are no fingers to give us prints has prevented us from identifying them," ventured one of the officers timidly.

"No corpse, no crime," put in Hamid. "All we find are human body parts."

The others present were eager to speak as well. Somewhat mollified by their enthusiasm, the chief of police listened attentively to what they had to say.

"The canvasses of the neighborhoods where the bodies were found produced zilch," said another officer. "Nobody heard or saw a thing. We don't have a single witness."

A psychological profiler said that his initial impression was that the perp would be an adult male, aged forty or under, educated, and employed in a decent job. "However, he's proud and aggressive. Perhaps he's taking revenge against the women in his domestic environment. This would be why he effaces their identity in order to put the police off his track."

"I'm more inclined to the idea that the killer hunts his victims randomly and that there's no link between them," said another officer.

Hanash rapped on the conference table, then put in forcefully, "We have to presume that either the perp is the same for both victims or the second perp was a copycat killer. Is there a link between the two victims? God knows. Did the perp, if the same, commit the second homicide as a means to cover up a clue to the first?" He paused, suddenly struck by the painful implications.

Alami looked at him anxiously and said, "Do you mean we have to wait for a third corpse?"

Perhaps I've taken my theorizing too far, thought Hanash. But he said in a bitter voice, "Somebody who covers up his first crime with a second could cover up his second crime with a third."

Alami extracted a cigarette but then quickly put it back in the pack and tossed the pack into the wastepaper basket. The others remained silent and shifted in their seats. They were not about to risk saying anything. Hanash set his small notepad on the table in front of him and spoke calmly and methodically, glancing down at his notes from time to time.

"First, the perp does not live in the neighborhoods where we found the body parts. We've combed the area. Our men have gone house to house questioning the residents, interrogating anyone who looked suspicious and pumping every doorman, parking lot attendant, shoeshine boy, and others for any information at all, however slight. We have an army of informants out there. If they haven't produced a scrap of information, it's because these murders were not committed by gangs, thieves, drunks, hash vendors, or dealers in hallucinogenic pills. Homicides of this sort are generally committed by an outwardly peaceful introvert who never meddles in other people's business and never draws attention to himself. Our informants are useless in such cases."

He flipped the page, glanced at the next, and continued: "Second, in both cases, the perp committed the homicide somewhere else and disposed of the parts that are useless to us in public places. As for the important parts—namely, the head and fingers—he disposed of them in a manner that would make it impossible for us to find them.

"Third, I believe that the perpetrator does not kill randomly. Was he acquainted with the two victims? Do we have anything to prove or refute such a connection? If the motive of the first murder was jealousy, revenge, or just suspicion of betrayal, the motive behind the second murder, using the same MO, might be similar or it could be to prevent the second victim from reporting something she knew about the first."

He paused with a sense of relief. He had just ventured all that he had. He looked Alami straight in the eyes and added, as though he had rehearsed it in his mind: "I recently checked back over all the homicides in Morocco that might fall under the heading of 'serial murders.' They're not many compared to Europe and America. In most cases, a second or third murder was committed out of fear of getting caught. The murderer is bound to make a mistake the next time, if he is indeed a serial killer."

He sat back in his seat and closed his eyes as though done with the matter and not interested to see the effect his remarks made on the others.

The chief said with alarm, "Does this mean we'll soon have another victim?"

Hanash responded in a self-assured voice, "I wish I knew where and when he'll strike next. The problem here is that our guy goes about his daily life normally, deceiving all around him because outwardly he's the same as everyone else."

Chief Alami's brow furrowed. He had to grant that Hanash's observations were realistic. In the language of the force, this meant assigning as many men as possible to the case. He'd have to recall all staff on holiday and put the police on high alert, all of which would cause stress, anxiety, and long overtime hours.

After the meeting, Hanash found Allal waiting for him outside his office. He seemed excited and eager to speak. Hanash ushered him into his office, indicated a seat, and grunted a welcome that meant "So, you finally showed up." But he remained silent as he contemplated the waste picker, who was even filthier than the last time. He smelled like he'd slept in a dumpster.

Allal spoke nervously. "I might have seen the guy who did it this time."

Hanash's eyes widened and gleamed as they remained pinned on the young man's face. He nodded approvingly, waiting to hear more. Allal fidgeted as though expecting a question.

"Go on. Talk. I'm listening," Hanash said.

Suddenly, Allal's attention seemed to wander. He yawned like someone waking from a restful nap. Squirming under Hanash's intense gaze, he muttered, "I said I *might* have seen him. That night, I saw this guy carrying a black plastic bag. He tossed it into a bin, but he pulled it out as soon as he saw me and rushed off."

"What did he do with it then?"

"Maybe he tossed it into the container where you found that . . . thing."

Hanash did a quick mental calculation. "What time was it?"

"Before midnight."

"Did you follow the guy?"

"I tried, but he got away."

"Was it a man?"

The question didn't require much thought, but the waste picker hesitated as though afraid to answer.

"Does it take such a long time to remember whether it was a man?"

Allal quivered, unable to speak.

"What did he look like, this guy?"

"Tall . . . but I couldn't make out his face."

"Why didn't you get in touch with me before this?"

"I only just found out what happened."

Now he had this Allal character sussed out. He had nothing useful to offer. The only reason he came to the station was to show that he was willing to serve and probably to get another pack of cigarettes.

5

HANASH'S INSTINCT PROVED RIGHT. THEY only had to wait a week to find the remains of another body. This time, the bag containing them was discovered far away from the previous locations and the victim was a male. Otherwise, it was the same MO: total dismemberment, excision of the reproductive organs, and removal of all possible identifying features.

Hanash never allowed anyone to interfere in his work; however, he had no choice but to bow to the order from central headquarters and agree to work with a SWAT team that had been sent down from the capital. He submitted to them the results of all his investigations and findings so far: a thick sheaf of papers containing about a hundred pages of repetitive routine reports.

The elite team spent a week sniffing for clues that Hanash's team might have missed, but came up with nothing. Nor could they find the slightest error, procedural shortcoming, or unexplored path in the work his department had done so far. After several meetings during the course of the week, the SWAT team leader took Hanash aside, smiled, and said with a trace of gallows humor: "Your work is spot on. Now all you have to do is catch the killer. Best of luck!"

There was something that Hanash hadn't shown the experts from Rabat: a study he had been putting together about serial killers in Morocco. A "serial killer" has been defined as a person who commits at least three separate murders with at least thirty-day intervals between them. The murderer is generally driven by some irrational compulsion, such as a desire to attract attention or a thirst for revenge. He applies the same modus operandi on all his victims, who have certain traits in common. According to psychological studies on the phenomenon, the victims' profiles help define about fifty percent of the killer's profile.

As the perp in this case had destroyed everything that might have made it possible to identify the victims, he had deprived the police of that fifty percent they need to set them on the trail. This was why Hanash decided to review the case files of the most famous Moroccan multiple murderers. They were not many and most of them only partially fulfilled the criteria of "serial killer."

They all came from poor and broken families and were victims, to varying degrees, of marginalization, depression, sexual repression, and drug addiction. Some had been sexually abused as children. All, without exception, had low levels of education and came from families that had recently migrated to the city, settled in its wretched slums, and suffered unemployment and destitution. This was certainly the case with Ghaffar

Aissa, aka al-Khanfouri, whose vocation was to attack weddings, rape and kill the brides, and disappear. The "Monster of Sidi Moumen," from Casablanca's most notorious slum area, cold-bloodedly slaughtered his whole family: his mother, his pregnant sister, and her son and husband. Another killer confessed to having committed six murders in less than a year by brutally striking their heads with a large stone. His savageness was rivaled by the notorious Abdelaâli Hadi, aka the "Monster of Taroudant." Himself molested during his adolescence, he exacted revenge by raping minors, nine of whom he killed, burying their bodies in the courtyards of abandoned houses.

Most of the other cases were of this sort. The murderer and the victims were all from the lowest strata of society. The exception was Mjinina, "the man with the severed head," who decapitated his victims, then would go into a bar, pull the severed head out of a plastic bag, set it on the counter, and order a beer for himself and another for the head.

But this case was different. None of Hanash's research shed any light on it.

Not so long ago, Hanash would have buried his frustration in drink and cigarettes. They would ease his troubles and lighten the burdens of life. But those habits ended after Officer Qazdabo came into his office, shot Hanash, and then shot himself. He also stopped surrounding himself with friends. He now preferred solitude and no more than the company of his own family and his dog.

He roamed from one street to another, trying to keep his mind occupied by something other than the atrocious murders. He wanted to be alone. As he walked, he began to single people out, boldly scrutinize their faces, and measure the degree to which they squirmed beneath his piercing glare. That was one of the tools of his trade. He'd use it against suspects, breaking them down, forcing them to backtrack and eventually to confess.

After over an hour of turning from one street to the next, he found himself near his daughter Manar's beauty parlor.

Rather than going on to university, Manar had decided to obtain a diploma in hairdressing. She loved her work and had many customers who called her salon "The Commissioner's Daughter."

His spirits soared when he realized where his feet had led him. The storefront with its bright neon sign saying "Salon Manar" filled him with pride. It had cost him a small fortune and he had to call in quite a few IOUs in order to obtain the deed for his daughter and outfit the place with the most modern equipment.

As it was nearly closing time, Hanash went to sit in a nearby café to wait for Manar to finish up.

Inside the salon, Manar was combing out the hair of one of her preferred clients. Her assistant was giving another client the full treatment in the hope of a generous tip. The assistant's client glanced down at her watch and said, addressing the entire room, "Have you heard about the latest murder? The killer butchered a man this time. He scattered the pieces all over the city."

"They haven't found the head or hands," added Manar's client excitedly. "They say that there are now six victims, five women and a man. The police are trying to keep the real number secret."

Manar's assistant said, "They found another body right here in Bernoussi."

"They say that they found another half a corpse in Ain Diab," said Manar's client.

The assistant's client said angrily, "Everyone's beside themselves with dread while the police act as though they're on another planet."

Manar's fingers cramped around the comb, which trembled in her hand. Should she tell them her father was in charge of the case? A wave of hatred welled up inside her. These silly women kept prattling on and on without the faintest idea of how hard her father and his men had been working. She wanted to scream at them, tell them right to their faces that they were a bunch of silly gossips and that because of these murders her father had been working around the clock. He didn't have a moment to spend with his family. He'd even stopped playing with his faithful friend, Kreet. Life at home had become hell, what with her father's nasty temper, and her poor mother constantly at the brink of tears and worn thin with worry. Their whole lives were run by that goddamned case, and all for the sake of the safety and security of the people.

Despite such thoughts racing through her mind, Manar smiled and said, "People are exaggerating. So far there have only been three murders, and the last victim was a man."

The other women's eyes flashed indignantly as they resumed trading the lurid details of imaginary crimes built from hearsay and hyperbole. They were only doing the same as everyone else in town. Social-networking websites were having their telltale effect. According to some, the killer was a religious fanatic who was waging a war against vice and wanton women. Others said he prowled the streets disguised as a woman in a burka, so the police now had female Salafis under surveillance. In some cartoons posted on the web, the killer was an elegant and cultivated man plagued by sexual impotence. Of course, "news" proliferated about dismembered body parts surfacing in other towns and cities.

After locking the door to her beauty parlor, Manar turned around and spotted her father across the street. He had never visited her at the salon before. He came over and gave her a warm hug as though he had just returned from a long trip abroad. Maybe there's some truth in the rumors, she thought.

"Where did you come from?" she exclaimed.

"Are you happy to see me?"

"Of course I'm happy. Ever since I can remember you've been too busy to spend much time with me."

Hanash glanced around quickly. "Let's walk for a bit. There's a café at the other end of the street. I'll treat you to a coffee and cake."

For a moment, she couldn't budge. She thought that he was trying to prepare her for some news. His hand disappeared inside his jacket, and she realized he was readjusting the position of his gun in its holster. She smiled weakly and said, "How's the case coming? Are you close to catching the killer?"

He hadn't expected this broadside from his daughter and suppressed a surge of anger. He had just spent a long time trying to free his mind from this case, if only for a little while. Then his daughter suddenly brought it up again and made him feel embarrassed at his lack of progress. To change the subject and lighten the atmosphere, he jested, "I'll report you to the police if you say anything more about that subject."

Manar was growing more and more suspicious of this behavior, which was so unlike her father.

"What's going on, Dad? Why did you come to see me?"

He cast her a pained expression. "Why are you giving me the third degree? Can't a father want to spend a little time with his daughter?"

But Manar couldn't control her curiosity or play along with her father's attempt to humor her. "Is everything really all right?"

"If I told you that I just wanted to take a little walk and have a cup of coffee with you after hours of boring meetings, would you believe me?"

She was silent for a moment, thinking, as they strolled along the pavement. It was turning twilight and there were few pedestrians around. Then she said, "You're the one who taught us that we should always be cautious because things aren't always what they seem." There was a profound sadness her voice, as though she too meant something else, something that troubled her deeply but that she was reluctant to tell her father.

He took her hand and squeezed it gently. "That isn't a rule written in stone," he said. "I'm wondering whether the reason you haven't married yet is because you suspect all men are guilty and should be thrown behind bars."

She laughed. "I don't look at it that way. But I don't want to get married just for the sake of getting married. Can I tell you a secret . . . or will you turn me in?"

He gritted his teeth. "No. . . . Word of honor."

She waited until after they took their seats on the veranda of a café and the waiter took their orders. Hanash looked at his daughter questioningly, trying to keep the detective glare out of his eyes.

"What's your secret, my dear?" he asked gently.

"You probably know what I want to say. We've already spoken about this subject, but only in jest. It's getting serious now."

Hanash frowned. He knew what his daughter was getting at. As he peered into her eyes he recalled the fond glances his handsome right-hand man would give her. It wasn't just loneliness that made Hamid spend so much time with the family after his mother died.

"Are you seeing him behind my back?"

"Of course not, Dad. . . . Well, only once. He didn't want to speak to you about this without knowing how I felt first."

"And how do you feel?" His hand rested on the table, unclenched.

"I won't tell you how I feel until I know your opinion."

Other fleeting encounters had followed. Hanash often invited Hamid over to discuss work or just to sit together in the garden and play with the dog. On such occasions, Hamid would exchange a few brief words, and many meaningful looks, with Manar. Her mother had picked up the signals. She even dropped a strong hint one evening when he had appeared at the door in a dapper black suit and freshly polished shoes, carrying a box of expensive chocolates. After he left, Naeema ventured that Hamid was practically doing cartwheels to win Manar's admiration and that he wanted to ask her out for a date, but feared the wrath of his boss.

Hanash smiled at his daughter, took a sip of his coffee, and said good-humoredly, "I should have had you followed. How could this have slipped by me?"

Manar gave him a pleading yet affectionate look. "Now, you promised me you wouldn't mention any of this to him. He respects you no end and he's easily embarrassed in front of you."

Hanash sighed and said, almost as though speaking to himself, "He's a decent young man. His main problem, though, is drink. He can't go to sleep unless he's had a few."

Manar looked down and blanched. She hadn't known that. Now she understood why her father hadn't encouraged it.

Hanash looked out toward the street and his eyes began to track a man in a long overcoat that was out of place in this warm weather. His mind turned to the killer, who was still at large, wandering freely among the people. At this very moment he might be plotting another crime. A brief gloom settled over their table as they were immersed in their private thoughts. Then Hanash looked up and asked, "Do you love him?"

The question stunned her. Her mouth widened into a bright smile that broke into laughter. She would never have expected her father to ask her such an embarrassing question. He added with an uncharacteristic delicateness, "I only want you to be happy, my dear. Hamid's not a bad sort. He can give up the drink, or at least drink in moderation. Actually, that part will be up to you now. As you know, I also used to have a drink now and then. And I smoked like a chimney. But a time comes when people change."

6

IF "WASTE PICKERS" REFERS TO the junk collectors who sift through garbage in the middle of the city, "scavengers" refers to those who live off the piles of urban waste after the city garbage trucks dump their loads at the huge landfill outside the city. Located about ten miles outside of Casablanca, the site, from afar, looks like a plateau. Nestled at its foot are a few wretched ramshackle villages whose inhabitants eke out their livelihood from refuse.

That morning, a scavenger was trying to shift a plastic garbage bag when it ripped open and a human hand poked through. The hand seemed to hang there, beckoning to him. He let out a scream and leaped back as though he'd received an electric shock. Then he tripped over another bag, which also ripped open, revealing a man's head, severed just below the chin. The eyes were wide open and seemed to beg for mercy.

The scavenger staggered, fell, and scrambled backward as he screamed for help. He was so terrified that he couldn't clamber to his feet. As his fellow scavengers rushed over, the air filled with a swelling wave of screams and howls as they too stumbled over plastic bags filled with human body parts.

Hanash was in the passenger's seat. Hamid was behind the wheel. They sped through the streets, the deafening siren clearing the way. The detective was sullen and withdrawn. He turned the malicious chain of events over and over in his mind. It was totally without precedent in the city and in his career. It had turned his job—his whole life—topsy-turvy. Never before had he felt such loss, confusion, lack of direction.

Hamid was equally silent. With Hanash in such a mood, he had no intention of venturing a conjecture. In fact, his mind wasn't really on the case. Yesterday, he had vowed to himself to bring up the subject of marrying Manar and he'd spent the whole of the previous night working out how to broach it. She'd rung him up and told him about her conversation with her father. They talked for more than half an hour. At one point, as delicately as she could, she brought up the one reservation her father had: the alcohol. Hamid almost burst out laughing when he heard that. Her father, before he quit drinking, used to think of Hamid as his favorite drinking buddy. At first, the young officer was new to alcohol and it was Hanash who'd invite him out for a chat over some drinks. Of course he didn't tell Manar this. Instead, he told her, in all sincerity, that he would be able to give up alcohol the moment they got married. Manar pretended to believe him, silencing the skepticism her father had instilled in her.

Now all notions of bringing up that subject with Hanash had flown out the window. The only topic of discussion in the coming days would be this new homicide. And wouldn't you know it, there went Hanash's phone, ringing insistently even before they reached the crime scene. The caller, moreover, was none other than the chief of police. Hamid knew this immediately from the way his boss glowered at the number on his mobile before answering.

"I do *not* want another failure!" Commander Alami snapped menacingly. "I do *not* want another corpse added to our growing list of cold files."

The police chief hung up before Hanash could say a word. Hanash pressed "end call" and flung his phone aside. Frustration and bitterness were written on his face. He turned to Hamid and said wryly, "He doesn't want another 'cold file.' If I don't get anywhere this time around, I'm going to ask to be taken off the case."

Hamid felt it wiser to keep his mouth shut, and remained silent until they reached the garbage dump. He parked the car a few steps away from the mountains of refuse with birds circling around them.

Since this area was outside the city limits, units from the royal gendarmerie and metropolitan police were added to the hodgepodge of police at the site. A crew from forensics wearing masks and rubber gloves were wading through the piles of garbage. Hanash forced himself to remain still for a moment. He appeared indifferent and aloof, but he was actually working out a game plan as he slowly scanned the scene. The head of the regional gendarmerie came up and greeted him warmly. They were old acquaintances. He took hold of Hanash's arm and steered him in the direction of where the CPD vehicles were parked. Hanash stopped abruptly, stunned by what he saw: seven black plastic bags lined up side by side. Flies buzzed around them.

"All these belong to the same victim?" asked Hanash in awe.

"Affirmative. The body was cut up into seven pieces. The head was packed in a bag of its own."

Hanash's eyes lit up. "Male or female?" he asked.

"Male. Mid- to late thirties, probably."

"Are all the parts there? Including the hands and fingers?"

"It's hard to confirm amid all this filth. But I believe so."

Hanash nodded. He looked around for his right-hand man and signaled him over. As Hamid came up, Hanash said excitedly, "It looks like this time we'll be able to ID the victim."

No sooner had Hanash returned to his office than Hamid entered, holding a printout of a picture he'd found on the computer.

"The face is identical with that of the severed head and the fingerprints are a match," said Hamid. "Rashid Abuela, thirty-five, unemployed, no police record."

The mother instinctively knew what the police were going to tell her the moment they knocked on the door of her modest home. She wasn't expecting good news. On the other hand, she had never imagined that someone would sever her son's head and dismember him, as the police put it.

"Why did she have to do that to him?" she wailed. "Why did she have to cut him into bits? Why did she hate him so much?"

She reeled, but Hamid caught her before she fell. Hanash called out for a glass of water. The last thing he wanted was for her to pass out, forcing them to wait until they could question her. As soon as she drank some water, Hanash asked, "Who is this woman you're talking about?"

The mother was unable to speak. Clutching her belly, she continued to weep and moan, her face contorted in agony and horror. She was barely aware of the circle of men hovering over her, waiting for her to speak.

Hanash appealed to her in a sympathetic voice. "Please, ma'am, tell us what you know."

She sat up, a sharp glint flashing in her eyes. "Who else would it be but that whore? The slut just wouldn't keep her claws off him. I'll kill her with my bare hands!"

"Her name and address, please," Hanash pressed her.

The mother burst into tears again and wailed, "Why'd she have to kill him just as his luck changed and he found a stable job and was about to get married?"

"Her name and address, please," Hanash asked again, impatiently.

"Fatma Zein. Seven years, she's been sucking his blood. Seven years!"

"Where does she live?" Hamid asked gently.

As soon as she told them the address, they left, as if making a getaway.

A riot of children playing in the street, gaggles of unemployed youth hanging out on the corners, a group of women collected in front of the public faucet, chitchatting as they waited their turn to fill their pans and buckets—this slum was notorious in Casablanca for its high rates of violence and endless neighborhood squabbles. It also had a reputation for having the highest rate of crimes related to hashish, vice, public intoxication, and other such offenses. Therefore, at the first sight of a police car, voices cried out, "Hanash!"—"Snakes!"—because that was the slang word for all policemen, not just the famed detective. Everyone vanished in a flash, including the women at the faucet. No one wanted to get picked up for arbitrary questioning. No family was without a relative or a neighbor who'd had some kind of run-in with the "snakes."

Hanash's car screeched to a halt. Another car carrying several CID officers pulled up behind it, followed by a police van filled with security guards. The guards leaped out and surrounded the building where Fatma Zein lived. When people saw that the police had homed in on a particular building, they began to reemerge and collect in the square. They were dying of curiosity. This raid meant something big.

Suad, the neighbor across the hall, watched from her doorway, propped against the frame in a sultry pose. In her mid-forties, she wore thick layers of makeup and blew and popped bubbles with her chewing gum in a flagrantly provocative way.

Hamid rapped on the door repeatedly until they heard an irritated voice calling from inside.

"I'm coming. I'm coming!"

Fatma flung open the door. When she saw the huddle of policemen, her jaw dropped and her eyes widened in alarm.

"Are you Fatma Zein?"

Unable to find her voice, she just nodded. An inspector elbowed his way inside and others rushed in after him. In a matter of seconds they had the place turned inside out. They upended every object, opened every drawer and closet, and strewed the contents about. Fatma shrieked at the havoc unfolding around her. Flinging her dyed blond hair away from her eyes, she cried, "I'm a respectable woman, gentlemen! Don't believe anybody who says otherwise. If people are going around saying nasty things about me, it's just because they want to get me into trouble with you."

When Fatma appeared in the hallway, arms locked behind her, with an officer on either side clasping her elbows, Suad threw Fatma a meaningful look, eyes sparkling with malicious glee. Outside, the guards struggled to restrain the large crowd of men, women, and children who were pressing forward to get a closer look.

A chorus of angry whistles and heckles arose, as always when there was a police raid and the "snakes" arrested someone from the neighborhood. Often the taunting would turn violent, with kids pelting the police with stones or smashing the windows of their cars, while others belted out slogans voicing social demands. The long-promised projects and programs to improve their living standards always evaporated after the electoral campaigns ended. Meanwhile, their despair and misery grew as they watched the rest of the city change and develop around them. Modern skyscrapers towered and commercial complexes burgeoned, their elegant façades lit up day and night, while their wretched neighborhood remained plunged in darkness.

Fatma was seated in Hanash's office. She was slumped in a chair, drained of energy, her face pale and her lips parched. Inspector Hamid sat opposite her while the detective was in the leather swivel chair behind his desk. After reading through the information he had just received on Fatma Zein, he looked up, fired off a few questions to confirm her identity, and then asked, "Do you have a record?"

She was startled by the question. She thought for a moment and then shook her head emphatically. "No. God forbid! I have no previous offenses, sir," she said.

He shot her a wry smile. "The report I'm holding here says that you do. You spent three months in prison for vice and drunk and disorderly behavior in a public thoroughfare."

"I was innocent, sir," she protested without looking at him.

Hanash's smile widened as he added, "And you were sentenced to pay compensation in a case involving a brawl with a certain Suad Muaddaba."

"She's the one who started it, sir."

Hanash's face hardened and he began to press her with questions: "What's your relationship with Rashid Abuela?"

Fatma's face reddened. "I . . . There is no relationship . . . not any more. Not since he told me he was going to get married."

"Do you know what happened to him?"

"No sir. And I'm still waiting to know why I'm here."

Hanash and his officer exchanged a long look. Then Hamid leaned forward, pushing his face directly in front of hers, and said forcefully, "We just found your lover in a garbage heap, hacked to pieces."

She emitted a loud gasp and flung her hand to her heart. "Oh my God!" she shrieked and burst into tears. She swayed forward and backward, slapping her knees and shaking her head hysterically, sending her hair flying in all directions.

It was hard to link that appalling murder to this wailing woman, but Hamid pressed on, more gently this time: "It was his mother who said you killed him."

"Don't believe a word she says! She blames me for her son's disappearance. She came to my home this morning, swore at me, and made the most appalling accusations. May God forgive her. I love her son and I only wish the best for him."

Hanash exchanged another meaningful look with Hamid. But before they could resume their interrogation, the door burst open and Suad pushed her way passed the guard. She was now in a tight djellaba that accentuated her curvaceous body. She'd braided her dark hair and added extra layers of makeup. One might have thought she had just entered a brothel rather than a police station. Fatma jumped in her chair. Her face contracted into a scowl as she turned to Suad and said in a crushed and defeated voice, "So you've come to get your revenge, Suad. Just remember that the Prophet, may peace be upon him, commanded us to care for our neighbors."

At a signal from Hanash, the guard withdrew from the room and shut the door behind him.

Fatma, momentarily forgetting where she was, added menacingly, "I'm warning you, Suad. You're going to regret what you're about to say."

"Shut your mouth," Hamid cut in. "And don't open it until I tell you to."

He then offered Suad a seat and said encouragingly, "Please speak freely. Tell us everything you know."

He turned to shoot a warning look at Fatma, who was about to protest.

As Suad began to speak, she eyed her prey with a defiant and gloating expression. "I saw Rashid come into our building yesterday, at about ten in the evening. About half an hour later, another guy showed up. I'd never seen him before. They partied until after midnight. Dancing, singing, drinking. The music was turned up full blast. You could just hear Fatma's screeches of laughter over the music. At about one o'clock I went over to complain. But just as I was about to knock, they turned the music down. God forgive me, but I began to eavesdrop. I heard things that I'll never forget as long as I live. The words still echo in my ears."

Fatma sucked in her breath. Her eyes widened as she stared at her neighbor with silent fury.

"What did you hear?" asked Hanash calmly.

"I heard her say, 'Just killing him doesn't give him what he deserves. Cut off his head and cut his body up into seven pieces. Then put them into seven bags. One for every year he tormented me.'"

"I said that?" Fatma shouted in a hoarse voice, pounding her chest. "You must have been dreaming!"

Suad ignored her. Looking at Hanash, she continued, "That's what I heard, sir. At first I thought she was joking. But the moment I heard Rashid had been killed and that they found his cut-up body in a garbage dump, I realized that it was no joke. So I came here to testify."

Fatma's face crumpled and her shoulders slumped. A shiver ran through her entire body. Hanash cast her a sympathetic look.

"Tell us what happened that night," he said softly.

Officer Hamid added gently, in order to encourage her, "It seems like you've been put through something horrible, and that's what drove you to do it."

The tears welled up in Fatma's eyes. She trembled and stammered at first. But when her features contorted into an expression of deep agony, Hanash and Hamid knew the mask was off. Her eyes grew vacant and for a moment it seemed as though she had given up caring about anything. After a silence, she began to speak with unexpected ease.

"I couldn't take it any more. The insults. The cruelty. Rashid was the love of my life. I loved him from the bottom of my heart. When he smiled, he brought tears to my eyes. I never tired of looking at him. I'd stare at him and never get my fill. I'd listen to him and long to hear more. It didn't matter how trivial. I'd cry when he was away and I'd cry when he was with me. I'd never loved anybody, not even myself, as much as I loved Rashid. Was I under some kind of spell? It's hard to deny. All my friends said I was. If only I could have fought his spell. It was so powerful. I lost all will of my own. I was blind. I was a slave to my love for him and ready to do whatever he said."

Suddenly, the meekness gave way to intense fury. A film clouded her eyes as though her mind had wandered elsewhere. But then she resumed in a venomous voice.

"Yes, I was ready to do anything for him. Anything! But he abandoned me. After seven whole years of sucking me dry, he dropped me. Just like that. Then, last week, he calls me up, invites me to a coffee on the beach, and says, 'Try to understand, Fatma. You know I can't marry you.' Of all the nerve! Then he has the gall to tell me that, now that he found a decent job, he wants to raise a family, but not with me!"

Her jaw worked furiously for a moment. Then she continued, staring vacantly into space. "I told him how I prayed for his happiness. 'May the good Lord grant you success,' I said. 'You have every right to build your future with the person dearest to your heart.' I asked him not to forget me. 'I couldn't take it if you put me out of your mind, just like that,' I said. He gave me that meek, lamb-like look that drives me mad and said he couldn't start a new life with another woman by cheating on her."

She swallowed with difficulty. A strange glimmer came into her eyes and her mouth twisted into a sneer. "I told him that I only wanted the best for him and I wished him all the joy in the world. Then I said, 'I have one last request before we part forever. Just spend one last night with me, a night that I'll cherish in my mind forever. Afterward I'll let you go and never bother you again.'"

Her mouth broadened into a triumphant smile. "He was that dumb. Dumb enough to agree to a hot night of sex with me as though I were some cheap whore. As though I hadn't been his lover for seven years. How cheap I must have seemed in his eyes. A despicable, groveling whore! I called up Maasoul the mechanic. He owns this car-repair shop. I knew that he was head over heels in love with me and ready to do anything I asked. I went over to his garage and smoked a joint with him. I only had to brush his cheek with a kiss to get him going. I told him that I would be his forever and at his service every single day if he just did me this one favor. I had him practically drooling over me. I let him fondle a lock of my hair as I told him what I wanted. He thought nothing of it, even after I spelled it all out in detail. 'Nothing to it,' he said. So I organized that party that Suad just told you about. The idiot

Rashid never suspected for a moment that I was planning my revenge, and in the most horrid way possible."

Officer Hamid spoke in a whisper so as not to stem the flow of her confession.

"Can you tell me where the mechanic lives?" he asked.

"La Ferraille," she snapped, annoyed at the interruption. "Where they sell second-hand car parts. Everyone there knows Maasoul."

Hamid slipped out of the room as Hanash nodded to Fatma to continue. She spoke with contempt and without a hint of remorse in her voice.

"Rashid was surprised when Maasoul arrived. He refused to drink. I started to dance for Maasoul in a really seductive way. I hoped to see just a tiny bit of jealousy in Rashid's eyes. I wanted him to feel offended that I was doing that right in front of him. I wanted him to get up and slap me. Or tell me to kick out Maasoul. Or show some desire for my body, if only for just one last time.

"Maasoul was getting turned on. He was plastered and beginning to lose it. Suddenly he got blindly jealous. That was how Rashid was supposed to feel! Before I knew it, Maasoul picked up a bottle and smashed it down on Rashid's skull. I didn't even have to give him the order! A single blow was enough make Rashid sag down against the wall, blood oozing from his head. . . . Maasoul yanked me to him and tore off my blouse. He swept all the plates and glasses from the table and made me lie down on it and fucked me right in front of Rashid's eyes.

86

"What hatred I saw in Rashid when our eyes met! I thought he'd leap up and drag Maasoul off me in one last fit of jealousy. But no. He drew in every bit of his last breath and spat at me.

"I grabbed the kitchen knife and stabbed him over and over, even though he was half dead. Then I cut off his head and I got drenched in his blood. I started to laugh. Then the devil whispered in my ears, 'Cut him up and fill up seven bags with his flesh and bones. A bag for every year you loved him like a fool.' That wasn't part of my agreement with Maasoul. Maybe he hadn't thought I was really serious about killing Rashid. Maybe he only acted out of drunkenness, lust, and jealousy. It took me a while to persuade him to help me cut up the body and put it in the bags. I think he started to think I was crazy at that point. He probably only obeyed me because he was drunk and still hot for me. He pulled me to him and kissed me hard. Then we got to work, hollering with laughter. We swore to keep this a secret, just between ourselves. We were evil. We kissed again and again, as we stuffed Rashid into the bags.

"I didn't like the idea of putting Rashid into the fridge. I poured a drink for Maasoul and said, 'I don't want Rashid to spend the night my house, even hacked to pieces.' Then an idea flashed into my mind. I said, 'We'll never get caught by the police if we make our crime look like the work of that serial killer the whole city's worked up about.' I told Maasoul about the bodies that the police keep finding in the dumpsters every night. 'The police will think it's the same killer,' I said.

The more we thought about it, the more we liked it. At dawn, we took the bags and put them in the trunk of his car, which was parked out in front. Then I went back inside, cleaned up the house, and slept all day long."

Maasoul put up no resistance when the police came to arrest him. He corroborated Fatma's account and all the pieces of the crime fell into place. But Fatma's idea of making it look like a continuation of the other murders complicated things. The chief of police ordered further investigation and closer questioning of Fatma and Maasoul to determine whether they had any connection to the other homicides.

Under the pressure of prolonged interrogation, which included various forms of physical and psychological "inducements," Fatma succumbed to a kind of stupor. She agreed to fabrications fed to her and didn't care how false the accusations leveled at her were. She even asked her interrogators to remind her of the details of her other crimes in case they'd slipped her mind. Maasoul, for his part, acted like someone who had just woken from a nasty dream. He'd respond to the interrogators with a stream of invective against Fatma. She was wickeder than the devil himself. She would probably get off and he'd have to pay for the crime alone, he thought. He figured that by confessing to other murders he'd make sure to drag her down with him. He, too, was struck by a fit of madness. He begged the investigators to believe him. He had a criminal record. He boasted of having been in prison twice.

*

Hanash wondered who in the force gave the press the impression that "tranquility" had been restored to Casablanca. He lifted his eyebrows at the front-page article in a respectable newspaper that cited him speaking about "cleansing the city of crime" and reassuring fellow Casablancans that they "could now sleep easy at night." He hadn't issued any statements to the press.

Chief of Police Mohammed Alami, on the other hand, convened a huge gathering of journalists from news outlets of all stripes so they could cover a reenactment of the crime of Fatma and Maasoul. Crime reenactments received nationwide TV coverage and the print media plastered their front pages with headlines and photos of them. It was great PR for the force and its vigilant heroes. It was little wonder, therefore, that the police chief's voice was filled with triumph as he stood before the cameras and spoke as though Fatma and Maasoul had carried out not one murder but four.

Later, during a meeting with Hanash, Alami gestured to a pile of newspapers and nodded approvingly. He must have noticed the skepticism in Hanash's face, because he asked, "Do you have any comments or objections?"

Hanash sat up in his seat. "I just want to say, sir, that so far we have nothing to prove that Fatma and Maasoul committed the three previous homicides. We're under enormous pressure from the public and the press. Everyone's eager to feel reassured. But on the three previous files, Fatma's and Maasoul's statements lack detail, they contradict each other, and there's no concrete evidence to support them. They've confessed to all charges without the slightest objection."

Alami folded his hands over his belly and said calmly, "It makes no difference. It's important to understand how much this case means to public opinion. I assume you care about that as well. I have complete confidence in your work. But at the same time, we have to calm the people down. If we tell them that the last crime is separate from the others, they'll only grow more alarmed. Rumors will proliferate and the press will criticize us and blow everything out of proportion. We have confessions. Even if there's no concrete evidence to support them, they're confessions all the same. That's an achievement in its own right. It should be publicized so people can be put at ease. Why don't you pick up some of those newspapers and read the headlines?"

Hanash did as he was told. Affecting a news anchor's voice, he recited: "'Killers Caught after Fourth Gruesome Murder.' 'Outstanding Success Relieves Casablancans of Fear.' 'Killers Arrested in Record Time Thanks to Outstanding Efforts of the Force.' 'The Criminals Are Behind Bars. Casablanca Safe and Sound Once More.'" Hanash looked up and gave the chief a look that acknowledged defeat. "It's hard to deny all that news."

7

IT WAS THE MORNING OF the first day of Eid al-Adha—the Feast of Sacrifice. Over two months had passed since the police had tied up the Rashid Abuela file. Hanash was in his garden, in his favorite chair, watching Hamid play with Kreet. Manar stole occasional peeks at Hamid from the balcony of her room. Hamid seemed happy and at ease, like one of the family.

Naeema had been bustling around the house since dawn. Eid al-Adha had a special sacredness for her. She began preparations a month beforehand. She'd have the walls repainted, buy new pots and pans for the kitchen, start obsessing about knives and sending them off to get them sharpened, and pester her husband with incessant demands. Now she was getting everything ready for the slaughtering of the sheep Tarek was fetching from a farm that belonged to a friend of his father's. That friend had been giving Hanash a sheep as a feast-day gift for years as an expression of gratitude for an old favor Hanash had performed for him.

Hamid laughed as he played tricks on Kreet. Hanash looked on as his mind strayed to the relationship between the officer and his daughter. He'd been giving a lot of thought to that matter during the past few days. His wife recently brought up the subject to him directly. He suspected that mother, daughter, and prospective groom were weaving plans behind his back because they were afraid he'd oppose an engagement.

In fact, Hanash had no strong objection at all. He just wanted to be absolutely certain, which is why he was awaiting the results of a thorough background check from the chief of Azilal, where Hamid grew up. Although Hamid now lived in Casablanca, he was not from there and not that much was known about his family and his upbringing. Of course, at some level, Hanash realized that this was his detective's mind working overtime. Everything he knew about Hamid confirmed that he was an honest and decent young man from a good family. His only flaw was his fondness for drink.

Now, as he watched Hamid playing with his dear dog, he felt a surge of affection for him. The inspector was actually his best friend after Kreet. He spent most of the day with him at work and thought of him as his right-hand man. He was the only officer in whom he felt he could confide his speculations and intentions in every case. Hamid, for his part, respected and obeyed his commanding officer. Ever since Hanash had returned to work after his scrape with death, Hamid was solicitous of his health and tried to keep him from overexerting himself.

Hanash wondered how it was that he'd never before thought of Hamid as the perfect match for his daughter. He vaguely recalled the inspector dropping hints, but he'd never caught on. Probably because he was used to talking to Hamid about suspects, investigations, and other work-related things.

Hanash leaned back in his chair, savoring the warm weather in the garden and the coziness of being at home with his family. He had to admit that he hadn't dedicated enough time to his family and that he had no close friends. Everybody seemed to shun him as though the only thing he had going for him was his ability to catch criminals.

At last, the gate to the villa opened and Tarek appeared together with the butcher. The two were pulling the sheep by its horns.

They all gathered around the bleating animal, exclaiming how fine it looked. Hamid's attention swiveled toward Manar, who was wearing a beautiful housedress. His eyes filled with admiration.

Hanash noticed how bright and bubbly his daughter was, laughing and giggling. As for Hamid, he seemed not quite there. Instead of stepping forward to help drag the sheep into the yard, he just stood with a grin on his face, holding Kreet by the collar.

"Are you going to slaughter the dog instead of the sheep?" Hanash asked as if upbraiding an officer at work.

Everyone burst out laughing. Hamid flushed with embarrassment as Manar flew to his rescue. Looking toward her father, she said, "Hey, officers, try to act for a moment like you're not at the station."

"That sheep looks like an ex-con," said Hamid timidly.

Hanash laughed. "What are you waiting for? Arrest it!"

"Yes, sir!"

Hamid leaped on the lamb and wrestled it into a position ready for slaughter.

Manar turned away, unable to stand the sight of blood. Once he'd finished his task, Hamid went over and stood beside her, offering her an apologetic smile as if to say that he, too, felt sorry for the sheep. She returned his smile, which encouraged him to furtively study her carefully arranged hair and the features of her subtly made-up face. He fought the temptation to allow his eyes to roam further.

Suddenly, the ringing of the house phone on the second floor pierced the air and mingled with the strident rings of Hanash's and Hamid's mobiles. The two men exchanged worried expressions as the cheerfulness around them evaporated. Only a work-related emergency could make all those phones ring at once. Hanash signaled to Hamid to answer first. No one budged until the officer finished listening to the caller. He hung up and said with a croak in his voice, "They want us downtown right away."

Hanash's eyes darkened. There was only thing that could drag them away from home and ruin the holiday with their families.

Hastening into the house, he went up to the second floor, out of earshot from the others, and rang the station. He listened, without saying a word, to the dreadful news the duty officer had to report.

He quickly changed his clothes, extracted his gun from its hiding place in the closet, and went back down to the garden. Everyone looked stunned, as though they had been struck by a curse. Hamid looked at Manar pleadingly as though to ask for forgiveness. Manar was in a daze, thinking about the life she'd have if she married a policeman.

Hanash had never felt as mortified as he did that morning of the first day of the feast. The body or, more precisely, the body parts were in a plastic bag that had been packed in a midsize cardboard box. That box was only three hundred steps away from the front gate of police headquarters, which was located on one of Casablanca's largest main boulevards.

Hanash stood glowering, arms folded helplessly in front of him. He was oblivious to forensics as they combed the ground, examined the box, took photos. In their astronaut-like costumes they looked like clowns, too clumsy to wallow through this bog of filthy murders committed by someone possessed by the devil. He stepped unsteadily toward the box and peered inside, then turned around and shouted furiously, "Did this lunatic decide to sacrifice a human instead of a sheep on this holy day?"

He backed away from the box, a grimace of disgust on his face, and cried, "He's challenging us! He leaves half a body right at the gate of HQ, in broad daylight on the morning of the feast. It's a travesty!"

A crime-scene technician came up and said, "The body's been severed into several parts. In that box, we have the head and the hands." He paused, wary of the detective's reputed sting. "However, the fingers have been cut off."

The detective nodded.

The technician, whose face had a sickly pallor, added, "The face has been so mutilated that its features are unidentifiable."

Hanash's lips curled. "He knows our work well. He's made sure we don't have a shred of evidence to work with."

His phone rang. He pulled it out of his pocket and answered without bothering to check who the caller was. It was the duty officer at headquarters. "They found another box at the Boulevard Brahim Rouhani traffic circle, sir."

That was only about half a kilometer from where Hanash was standing. He headed over on foot.

A policeman was guarding the box. Next to him stood an elderly man who obviously didn't belong to the police. There weren't enough men on duty today, it being a holiday. Most other members of the force had the day off and were gathered around feast tables.

Hanash glanced inside the carton and saw the lower half of an adult male. It had been severed from the torso in the same nauseating way as the other victims. He stepped back, his expression a mixture of revulsion and despair. Again, the murderer had left them nothing to go on, nothing to give them hope.

Just then, the vehicles from CID, CPD, and forensics screeched to a halt in the traffic circle and disgorged their assorted personnel. As the team from forensics got to work, the detective turned and contemplated the old man who was standing next to the police guard.

"Who's he?" he asked the guard.

"He's the guy who reported this carton. He sells cigarettes by the piece, across the street."

Hanash eyed the old man like a hunter who had spotted a valuable prey, and watched the man's face turn to terror under his gaze. He opted for a courteous tone: "Please tell me what you saw. I'm the detective in charge here."

The old man's face sagged wearily. He had the doleful, sunken eyes of an abandoned child, but his voice was filled with infinite venom against the man who had committed these crimes.

"I was over there on the other side of the street. A taxi stopped right here and a man got out. I couldn't make him out clearly. He took two cartons off the roof of the car and set them down on the pavement so that he could pay the driver. He picked up one carton—by the way he lifted it I could tell it was heavy—and headed off, leaving the other box right where it was. After he'd left, this box here began to arouse my curiosity. I thought the guy would come back to get it after delivering the first box. But he was taking such a long time. I crossed the street and sort of circled around this . . . prank of the devil. I was just curious, I swear. I didn't intend to steal anything. May God be my witness! I stooped down and tore off the tape. When I opened the box I saw the plastic bag. As soon as I opened that, I stumbled backward and fell on my behind and started to scream. Then I got up and ran to the police station and told the policeman there what I saw."

Hanash was shocked by the information he'd just received. The killer didn't own a car. He had the audacity to transport the body on the roof rack of a taxi. But still, that meant he couldn't live too far away. Or at least not outside the city limits. He'd have to find a taxi and there wouldn't be many around this Eid al-Adha morning.

"Did you take down the taxi's license plate? Did you notice what kind of car it was?"

"No, sir. I was on the other side of the street and my eyesight's not good."

"So you couldn't see the face of the guy who took the boxes down from the taxi?"

"No, sir. And that's the truth, so help me God."

Just as Hanash was about to ask another question, he heard a field technician from forensics clearing his throat to catch his attention. Hanash turned to him.

"Yes?"

The technician confirmed what Hanash had already expected.

"This carton contains the lower half of an adult male. Unfortunately, the genitalia have been amputated."

Another technician came over and showed Hanash a piece of folded paper with some bloodstains on it.

"We found it at the bottom of the box, stuck between the thighs."

Hanash's eyes lit up at this unexpected tidbit. "Take care of the prints, if there are any. I want the results from the lab ASAP."

Hanash heard his phone in his pocket just as he was about to enter the meeting room. As he'd suspected, it wasn't the chief. Alami had been using his own sources to keep up to speed. He had been avoiding Hanash because he knew the first thing he'd hear was the detective repeating that the last homicide was different from the others, yet the police had gone ahead and pinned the whole lot on Fatma and Maasoul anyway.

The caller was Naeema. She searched for words that she hoped would sound more sympathetic than reproachful. "The grill's ready. I just wanted to know if you and Hamid were going to make it for lunch."

Hanash gave a bark of laughter. "Ask Manar if she still wants to get married to a policeman," he said wryly.

Naeema winced because Manar was standing right next to her. In the same wry tone, she said, "Ask her yourself. She's right here." When Manar refused to take the phone, Naeema added, "Why should she turn down what I accepted?"

Keeping up the sarcasm, Hanash said, "Who's the one who had to accept all this?"

Softening her voice, she said, "I'm not as sorry for myself as I am for you, who was torn away from your family on the day of the feast."

He appreciated her effort to strengthen their bond but still, from the tone of her voice, he sensed the tears in her eyes.

Hanash was the type of man to keep his feelings to himself. But in the past few days, as he worked up to give his consent to his daughter's engagement, he'd begun to feel that his ideas and attitudes were changing and to regret how gruffly he'd treated his wife at times.

As Hamid watched Hanash enter the meeting room, head bowed and lost in thought, he knew his boss was troubled and that it didn't all have to do with work.

The room was packed, as all officers had been ordered to report in. Hanash took his place in front of them and spoke with compassion.

"I know that your place—and mine—should be with our families today, on this first and holiest day of Eid al-Adha. We should be gathered around our dining tables with our loved ones, feasting on grilled meat and drinking copious amounts of tea."

He paused as he turned to the business at hand. "As I have believed from the start, the homicide committed by Fatma and Maasoul had no connection to the three previous ones. As we know from their testimony, Fatma and Maasoul deliberately copied the MO of the others in order to mislead us. Today, we're looking at the fourth murder by the original perp. This time, he's openly taunting us. He's laughing in our faces. He

brought his victim right to our doorstep. He deposited it virtually gift-wrapped at the entrance of the biggest police station
in town. That was his Feast Day gift to us."

He observed the bitter smiles on the faces of his audience.
They too were stung by the insult. He resumed, in a stern
voice, "The killer is familiar with our methods, as we know.
But this time, he presented us with some information. First,
he took a taxi, so he might not own a car. Second, we have
a witness who at least saw the killer from afar. Accordingly,
we can be fairly certain that he is indeed male and that he
works alone. Third, we have a taxi. If we can identify it, we
have a potential witness in the driver. Fourth, forensics found
a piece of paper in the second carton. They're analyzing it
at the lab as I speak. Let's hope it yields something useful.
Fifth, chief medical examiner Dr. Amrani has volunteered to
try to reconstruct the face of the last victim from what's left of
it. Hopefully it will serve as a facial composite to ID the victim. Last, there's the matter of the psychological profile of the
murderer. What were his motives? Why did he carry out these
murders in this particular way? Is this a serial killer driven by
some thirst for revenge? Or is this a multi-victim murderer
who just kills as a kind of hobby? Every team knows what it
has to do. We're in a race against the clock. The killer must
have overlooked something. Our mission now is to find it."

The hunt for the taxicab proved a letdown. Without a license
number or even a description of the car model, it was an

almost impossible task. Hanash had his own views about taxi drivers when it came to the police. They never came forward with useful information because they feared constantly being dragged back to the police station to be questioned in connection with a case or to be asked to identify a culprit of some sort. Worse, they could end up being summoned to appear in court as a witness and end up losing many days of income. So they adopted an "I-know-nothing" attitude to preempt such headaches.

Because of the unprecedented spate of homicides, Hanash had been in frequent contact with Dr. Amrani, the chief medical examiner. In fact, by now he'd spent so much time at the morgue that he found he could stay focused on the remains of the victim without feeling queasy while she discoursed on the nature of the injuries and how they were inflicted. After she'd invited him to the morgue to demonstrate how systematically the murderer had destroyed the facial features of the last victim, he was doubly impressed at her explanation of how she had begun to reconstruct the face using a type of sculpture technique, building outward from the shattered skull, aided by forensic photography and computer graphics.

This is not to suggest that he abandoned his long-held skepticism on the value of forensic science—he continued to favor the old-fashioned gumshoe approach of tracking villains clue by clue. But he still held out hope that the forensic evidence technicians—the "FETs," was that what they called themselves now?—would come up with something useful.

Therefore, the moment they called, Hanash raced over to their premises, praying for a lead connected with that folded piece of paper they'd found in the second carton.

The forensic graphologist was a short man in blue overalls that made him look like an automobile mechanic. Hanash had never met him before. He had never needed a handwriting expert in his previous cases. Holding the paper with a pair of tweezers and extending it toward Hanash so that he could see it, the graphologist said, "It's torn out of a school notebook . . . a handwritten letter, unsigned."

He brought the letter beneath the concentrated light of a magnifying lamp and recited with a quiver of excitement in his voice:

"To whom it may concern,

"I avenged myself against him in this way because he exploited my harsh circumstances, destroyed my honor, and ruined my future. That is the reason for what has occurred."

The expert then embarked on a discourse about how useful handwriting was in character analysis. "It provides the best documentation of a person's nervous constitution," he said.

He spoke confidently, as though giving Hanash a lecture. "I can tell by the rounding of the angles of certain letters and the more exaggerated loops in others that the writer is mimicking a more feminine style of writing, probably to make it seem like the letter was written by a woman. It is inconsistently done, lending further weight to the premise that the writer is actually male. Moreover, he is aggressive, introverted, and quite well educated. Note how he pressed so hard on the paper that you can see some of the letters in relief on the back. He was clearly anxious and the pen did not have enough ink."

The graphologist then digressed into a lengthy and abstract discourse on the spiritual aspect of writing and the art of calligraphy in Arab culture.

Hanash closed his eyes as anger welled up. He burst out, interrupting the expert: "This letter is just a decoy. He wants to trick us into thinking the killer's a woman! He's doing everything he can to mock and ridicule us. He must have known how he inspired Fatma to stage a copycat crime. Now he's taking advantage of Fatma's crime just as she'd taken advantage of his. He's giving her a wink of recognition." Hanash added, as though stating the obvious, "Of course, he left no fingerprints or identifying marks on the letter."

At that moment, another technician appeared and, in a voice raspy from excitement, said, "Please come with me. I found something of interest on one of the cartons."

They hurried after him to another lab, equipped with microscopes, computer consoles, and other scientific instruments and machinery. Indicating the carton in which the torso of the last victim was found, the technician spoke, taking care to assume the appropriate scientific detachment.

"According to our analyses, one bloodstain on this carton doesn't match the blood type of the victim."

"It must be the killer's blood," the first technician said.

"Pursue this matter further. You're doing great work."

Hanash could hear the hollowness in his own voice as he said that. This discovery did nothing to encourage him. He was not belittling the work of the technicians or the forensics department as a whole. In his experience, however, their work was painstakingly slow. Then, in the absence of a suspect, what good was a drop of blood or a specimen of handwriting? With what could they compare them so as to yield a definitive deduction? He needed the beginning of a thread to grasp, and he needed it now so he could figure out what steps to take next. He felt like shouting at them: "You should be thinking of the woman whose handwriting the killer faked. Maybe she played a part in his life."

He began to review the letter in his mind. It mentioned "vengeance" outright. It talked about a motive: "exploitation" of circumstances, "harsh" position, violation of "honor." It blamed the victim. Hanash had copied the text of the letter, and he read it over a few more times. Then, as though speaking to himself, he said, "The author of the letter is definitely male. He is introducing himself to us, telling us his motives and explaining the part the victim had to play. But the victim this time is a man and the 'honor' the letter speaks of refers to the killer's honor. Could it be that the victim had betrayed the killer in some way? Had an affair with his girlfriend or wife? We know now that we're looking at a dish whose main ingredients are vice and vengeance."

He put on a pair of gloves, picked up the carton in which the letter was found, and examined it closely. He turned it over and over. It was a midsize carton made of thick cardboard. He noticed some Latin letters and numbers affixed to the carton here and there. Taking out his notepad and pen, he copied them:

cla – d oss ier b-t-45pes

One of the technicians noticed what he was doing and said, "We're still working on what those letters mean. It looks like they're taken from different stickers and affixed randomly, in no particular order."

8

NOT A DAY WENT BY without Hanash working long overtime hours at the station. Not a night went by without him tossing and turning in bed, fretting about the case. The murderer had intentionally left them some fragments of clues this time. He had even brought the body virtually to the door of police headquarters. It was pure audacity. But that may have been his way of saying that he was tired of killing and that he longed for the police to catch him now that he had shown how his superior intelligence could outwit them.

In that letter he left, he offered them a rough sketch of what had driven him to such brutality: love and betrayal. Why divulge that?

Yet, despite his generosity in giving them this information, he still took sufficient precautions to keep them off his scent. He'd left nothing that investigators could really take hold of. He chopped his victim into pieces. He savaged the face so brutally as to make any visual identification impossible. He cut off the fingers, so no fingerprints. How long did all that take him? Where did he perform these vile acts? Was he high on drugs or alcohol? Or clearheaded and alert? In his letter, in the voice of a woman betrayed, he established that he had a right to avenge himself in this manner, which was even more brutal than his previous crimes, with a mutilated face delivered to their door. How was he related to the victim? Was he a relative? A friend? Or was it just bad luck that threw the victim in his path?

He also knew that, with every day that the killer remained at large, the case grew more impenetrable and the perpetrator grew more elusive, like a bird flying into the distance until it vanished from sight.

He thought back to his study of previous serial murderers and the like. If there was one element they had in common it was that they all claimed at least five victims. Police were only led to the "Monster of Taroudant," the child molester and murderer, after he had struck for a ninth time. Some killers committed so many murders that they lost count of their victims. But never before had a murderer left a letter to the police or destroyed the remains of his victims in order to conceal their identity. All previous incidents were driven by rage and revenge, in contrast to the systematic dismemberment in the current cases. The grim reality was that, with so little to go on, the police might have to wait for yet another homicide, in the hope that the perpetrator would slip up as he grew cockier and more reckless. It occurred to Hanash that this new-style Moroccan serial killer had been influenced by *Seven* or *The Silence of the Lambs* or other such films. In fact, anyone could read online about the many real-life American serial killers who would send the police either a part of their victim's body or coded letters or, in some instances, would even call up the police in person. Such ruses were all part of a demonic cat-and-mouse game the killer played with the police in order to prove his superior intelligence. The notorious "Zodiac Killer" made Hanash's blood run cold. He claimed thirty-seven victims, yet his identity remained unknown and he remained at large even though he sent coded letters to the police after each murder. Despite all the advanced technology and advances in cryptology at their disposal over the years, American law-enforcement agencies had been unable to crack the Zodiac Killer's codes. Then there were the spine-chilling Donald Henry "Pee Wee" Gaskins, who was only apprehended after having committed eighty to ninety murders, and Harold Shipman, aka "Dr. Death," who murdered over two hundred patients under his care. Less prolific but more grisly was Ted Bundy, kidnapper, rapist, and necrophile, who went on killing sprees in seven states in the US.

The more Hanash read about serial killers abroad the more he suspected that the guy who was eluding him belonged to that category. Previous cases in Morocco were all simple illiterates. Some murdered members of their own families, while others were vagabonds. A few were highway robbers, like Abdelali Amer, aka "the Savage," who beat his victims to death with a rock after robbing them. In all these cases, the killers remained in hiding or on the run; none intended to defy and play games with the police. But the culprit Hanash was dealing with was of a different order. He was educated and intelligent, and used more sophisticated methodsO. At the same time, he was probably driven to fulfill some psychopathic compulsion; he may not have even been personally acquainted with his victims.

This possibility led Hanash to consider other cold files in areas outside his jurisdiction. Could they have been committed by this guy using different methods? Could they have contained coded messages that the investigating officers had not caught on to?

Naeema was woken again by her husband's tossing and turning. He was babbling incoherently in his sleep.

Unable to calm him with words, she stroked his head and recited Quranic verses to ward off evil: "Say: *I seek refuge with the Lord of mankind, the King of mankind, the God of mankind . . .*"

He seemed feverish. She laid a hand on his forehead.

"From the evil of the sly whisperer who whispers evilly into the hearts of men . . ."

Suddenly, Hanash shot out of bed and began to rummage through the closet. Naeema sat up in alarm. He's delirious, she thought. He looked over his shoulder and told her in a natural, fully awake voice, "Calm down, dear, I just remembered something."

Fishing his notepad out of his jacket pocket, he flicked through it until he found the page where he'd copied down the ciphers he'd seen in the lab.

Naeema came up behind him, put her arms around him, and placed a kiss on his shoulder. "These murders are going to drive you mad. Why don't you ask to be taken off this case?" she pleaded.

He removed her hands gently. "I'm going to take a stroll around the garden," he said as he hastened out of the room holding the notepad.

In the hallway, he noticed the light from beneath Tarek's bedroom door. As usual, his son was up at all hours fiddling about on his laptop. He knocked on the door and slipped into the room quickly, as though afraid his wife might be at his heels.

Tarek craned his neck to look behind his father to ensure he wasn't fleeing some danger. His father was wheezing and his face was dark and brooding. He looked like he'd been punched. Hanash set his notepad on Tarek's desk and said wearily, "Take a look at these. Can you make anything out of them?"

Sensing his father's anguish, Tarek bent toward the notepad while Hanash took a seat at the edge of his son's bed.

"As long as you spend all your time on the internet," Hanash said, "have a look to see if it comes up with anything about those numbers and letters. They were written on the carton in which we found half a body. The technicians at the crime lab dismissed them as nonsense but I'm not convinced. It might give us a lead."

Tarek spelled out the cipher in an awestruck voice: "Cla – d oss ier b-t-45pes . . . What could it mean?"

He looked over at his father, who sat bent forward, his head resting on his hands, staring blankly in the direction of his feet.

"They're just numbers and letters, Dad. Maybe they were torn off from something else. Or maybe the perp means to challenge us with a riddle."

Hanash stood up with a dismissive flick of his hand as though to say he had changed his mind and tell his son not to bother.

"Hey, Dad, I'll give it a go," Tarek called out as his father left.

Tarek swiveled back to his computer. He created a new document, typed in the mysterious letters and numbers, and gave it a title in a large bold font in red: "The Butcher of Casablanca."

Beneath this he wrote: "Investigation assigned to: Tarek, son of Head of CID Detective Mohamed Bineesa, aka "Hanash."

In addition to studying for the police academy entrance exam, which he planned to take after law school, Tarek was an avid reader of detective novels and an addict of TV crime serials and films. He was also saturated with the investigative climate at home. Often he'd question his father about his work and his father wasn't stingy with information. In fact, when he had the time, Hanash enjoyed explaining to Tarek certain legal procedures or clarifying points his son found confusing. Occasionally, he'd lay out the details of a case and have his son marshal the evidence that could convict the defendant.

The late-night hours were Tarek's favorite time for surfing the net. He liked to keep up to date with the latest criminal investigative methods and try to solve crimes. Sometimes he'd get distracted and might even sneak the occasional peek at a porn site. But the task his father had given him was a kind of game and it set a challenge he could not resist tackling. He was prepared to spend the whole night at it, face to face with his computer. He had no plan to start with, being in totally unmarked territory. He merely began rearranging the letters haphazardly.

As he burned the midnight oil wrestling with this puzzle, he felt he caught a glimpse of his what his father was dealing with: looking for a needle in a haystack. His dad was always so hard on himself and spent hours at his office working until late at night, depriving himself of any pleasure or relief as he banged his head against a brick wall.

Tarek found it thrilling that the number 45, plus those random letters, might lead to the killer who'd been terrifying the city. Once in a while he'd get exasperated, ready to throw in the towel and climb into bed, but some sense of urgency spurred him on and kept him awake. His mind was ticking, his senses were primed, and he was determined to win a prize that he could hand his father over breakfast.

A plan of action formed in his head. He discarded the 45 and studied the remaining letters. Surely they couldn't all form a single word or a meaningful sentence. He decided to try his luck with fewer letters. After a number of unsuccessful tries, seven letters gave him a real word: "dossier," the French for file or a folder containing files, though it could also mean backrest or the back of a chair.

Now, what about the rest of the letters—b, t, es, p, cla—plus the 45? He arranged and rearranged them in numerous meaningless combinations. Just as he felt he'd reached a dead end, another idea occurred to him: perhaps two or more of these letters formed an abbreviation.

He passed his tongue over his parched lips and began to separate and reorder the letters again. After a few more tries, he placed the "p" after the "es," giving "esp"—the abbreviation for Spain: Espagne.

He stared at that "esp" as though he finally had something valuable in his grip. "Spain" had to be the meaning. But he couldn't take it further without figuring out what the rest of the letters meant. True, he had "dossier," but that had various meanings. He took the remaining letters—cla b-t—and tried rearranging them. Then he added the 45 and tried to affix them all to what he already had. He produced the following permutations:

CLA-DOSSIER B-T-45ESP
B-T-CLA-DOSSIER-45ESP

CLA B-T DOSSIER 45ESP
DOSSIER CLA-B-T-45ESP

That, he thought, would be enough for starters. He typed the first two combinations into Google. No hits. He typed in the third. Before pressing "search" this time, he closed his eyes, muttered a brief prayer, and then clicked the mouse. A whole page unfolded on the screen before him with information about the Agencia Limitada Commercial Buzón. He opened a new tab in the browser, opened Google Translate, selected Spanish to French, copied and pasted in the Spanish text, and came up with: Agence commerciale limiteé des boîtes à lettres. He mouthed the words, his lips trembling in excitement. He discarded "DOSSIER" since it bore no relation to anything and must have been inserted as a kind of decoy. He called out to his father.

When his father came back into the room, Tarek pointed at his screen and said, "This is a Spanish company that exports mailboxes."

Hanash's eyes widened. He pulled up a chair next to Tarek and the two began to search for everything they could find about that Spanish firm. At last Hanash's morale began to pick up. The murderer had taken his game of toying with the police to a higher level. He had given them a kind of anagram. They were now left with the letter "T" and the "45." They were unable to make sense of them yet, but perhaps their significance would emerge later.

Tarek stood up, yawned, and stretched. He felt dizzy and unable to concentrate any more. He needed to sleep. But Hanash had a sudden flash of inspiration.

"Send them an email and ask who they deal with here in Morocco. Ask them if there's a particular firm that they've franchised to distribute their products."

"Do you think they know French? The Spanish are famous for speaking only Spanish."

"All Spaniards who invest in Morocco know French. Let's give it a try. We got nothing to lose."

Tarek applied himself to the task, vowing to get his fill of sleep afterward, and wrote the company an email asking who they worked with in Morocco. Despite the late night, he was up early to check his emails—and to his surprise, they had already replied. It was essentially a form letter, in precise and courteous French, that opened with an expression of gratitude for the confidence the recipient had placed in the company's products. It concluded with the name and address of the sole distributor of their products in Morocco: al-Saada Co., Ltd., in Casablanca.

Hanash fetched his phone from his bedroom and dialed, his eyes fixed on the computer screen. "Good morning, Hamid. Are you at work yet? On your way. Good. Turn around and pick me up at home. You'll find me waiting at the gate."

Tarek thumped his chest proudly and said, "Confess! Confess! I helped you out!"

Hanash smiled as he hastened out the door and said, "You spend all your time at the computer doing nothing productive. At least this time you did something useful."

Tarek rushed after his father, caught hold of his arm, and shouted, eyes glistening with a glee he hadn't felt in years.

"You got to pay up!"

Naeema rushed into the hallway, eyes wide in alarm.

"What's going on?"

Hanash winked to reassure her and said, "You stay there, Naeema. This is between men."

Tarek made more demands: "You owe me one pair of sneakers in exchange for the services I performed for your department."

"Hah!" his father scoffed. "The department doesn't even pay us for overtime, so why should it pay you? Anyway, what do you think happens next? It's not as though the perp's going to be waiting to greet us at that company's front door."

As Tarek turned to return to his bedroom, he cocked a finger at his father and said, "We'll see about this later." He gave a loud yawn and shut the door behind him.

Hamid's enthusiasm flagged as he listened to Hanash relate his early-morning discovery. As the detective spoke, Hamid kept his eyes on the road and refrained from comment. He suspected that a good part of the detective's excitement stemmed less from his conviction in his new lead than from his pride in his son who'd discovered it.

They had no trouble finding the company. It was located in the industrial zone in an unremarkable building with a no-frills façade and a utilitarian entrance. They were received by a person who introduced himself as Aziz Habbab, head of personnel. He could tell they were high-ranking police officials before they introduced themselves. He led them into a large meeting room because his office was too small, and tried to check the trembling in his hand as he gestured to them to have a seat. They remained standing.

"Undoubtedly you know who we are?" Hamid asked, his eyes fixed intently on Habbab's face.

"You're police, sir. Who wouldn't recognize Detective Hanash, whose photographs appear frequently in the newspapers and on the internet?"

Hanash smiled as though detecting a familiar ruse. "Your company imports products from Spain. Could you tell us what they are?"

Habbab knitted his brow. "Our company is the only company exclusively licensed to import mailbox units from the Spanish firm Agencia Limitada Commercial Buzón."

Hanash gave Hamid a nod that indicated "You see, Tarek was right," then turned back to Mr. Habbab. "And who are your customers here in Casablanca?"

The man took a cigarette lighter out of his pocket and began to fidget with it. "We have a lot of customers," he said, stammering slightly. "Most of them are building contractors. But we have some ordinary customers, too."

"Could we see a sample of those mailboxes?"

Habbab noticed the strange gleam in Hanash's eyes and was deeply intrigued to know what the purpose of this visit was, but was too afraid to ask. He nodded and led them down a long corridor that opened onto a huge warehouse stocked with hundreds of cartons. Hanash moved past the manager and examined one of the cartons. It looked exactly like the one in which they had found the last body. He turned to Hamid, eyebrows raised.

Hanash noticed that every carton had the characters "T45" printed on them. Now that was interesting. "What does this T45 signify?" he asked Habbab.

Looking back and forth between the two officers, the manager replied, "T means unit. So each of these cartons contains forty-five mailboxes of the sort you find in the foyers of apartment buildings."

So that was the last piece of the puzzle solved, thought Hanash.

Officer Hamid narrowed his eyes at the man and said, "Open the box."

Habbab quickly did as asked. He pulled back the flap to reveal the mailboxes stacked inside. The inspector took one out and examined it from different angles. They were well made, elegantly finished, and clearly designed for upmarket apartment blocks. He exchanged glances with Hanash, then glared at Habbab again.

"Did you give empty cartons to anyone?"

"No, sir." The personnel manager was visibly trembling.

"I want an empty one of these boxes," Hanash commanded.

The company employee removed the mailbox units from one of the cartons and set them to one side.

"I also want a list of your customers here in Casablanca."

"In my office . . . I'll give you whatever you need."

They returned through the corridor and stopped before the frosted-glass windows of Habbab's office. As Habbab opened the door, he asked, "Don't I have a right to know the reason for this search?"

"Did you hear about the murder that happened on the first day of the Eid?"

Habbab's eyes widened and his hand went to his chest. "Dear Lord! Of course I heard of it. The whole town's talking about nothing else!"

"The body was severed into two halves. Each half was cut up and put into one of these boxes."

The man gasped and the color drained from his face. His pale lips worked as though trying to say something, but nothing came out. Hanash pinned him with a probing stare and asked, "How did these cartons fall into the hands of the killer?"

"It's impossible for one of these cartons to leave the premises empty." Habbab's terrified eyes rapidly shifted back and forth between his interrogators.

Reading his boss's mind, Hamid pressed his face closer to Habbab's face, let a few seconds tick by, and then fired: "Perhaps you know the killer."

The man jumped, but he fired back angrily: "I don't know anyone who could kill!"

Hanash shot out, "Or maybe it was you."

Habbab laughed. The two officers were trying frighten and confuse him. That much he knew. He smiled feebly, shook his head as though to say he'd never heard anything so absurd, and muttered, "God protect me from the accursed Satan."

Hanash had not seriously suspected the man. It was part of his technique to rattle people in order to keep them on the defensive.

Hanash took the list of customers and started to read it, starting from the last entry.

"Your most recent client was the Manar building. In Lafayette?"

Hamid jumped in excitedly. "I know that building! It's a tall and luxurious-looking office block. I don't think it's completely finished yet."

The company employee, relieved that he was no longer under pressure, stepped in to correct him. "It is finished. Otherwise they wouldn't have ordered the mailboxes."

Hanash eyed the man closely. The short and thickset Mr. Habbab was now calm and unflustered. An unfurrowed brow and candid eyes told Hanash that the man had nothing to do with this case and did not have the constitution of a murderer. With a quick nod, he signaled Hamid that it was time to go. They quickly headed out of the building and to their car.

As the car sped out of the industrial zone, Hanash said, "I think we got something solid this time. At least we finally have a causal connection between a point 'a' and a point 'b.'"

"I suspect that that personnel manager was hiding something from us," Hamid said.

"In any case, we'll have to go back to that company if we don't get anywhere," Hanash muttered as he became absorbed in thoughts.

Hamid too fell silent. It was pointless to discuss this further before they had more information to go on.

They pulled up in front of the Manar building, which was located on one of Casablanca's main boulevards. Hanash was struck by the coincidence that the building bore the same name as his daughter.

It was an impressive building: nine stories tall, with a façade of dark smoked-glass panels set in a grid of shiny metal beams. A small, well-tended garden with flowerbeds separated the building from the street. It was clear that the major construction had been completed, but it was still unoccupied and the office spaces had not yet been put up for sale.

Officer Hamid pressed the doorbell next to the glass front door. He pressed again and listened, but no sound came from within. He gave the door a few tugs and shoves, but nothing gave.

Hanash, squinting up at the rows of closed windows, said, "There's nobody here."

They turned to head back to the car. Just then, the front door of the building opened and a young man appeared wearing a blue private security guard's uniform. He hesitated for a moment and then called out, "Were you the guys who rang the doorbell?"

They turned in surprise. Hanash gave him a quick once-over: early twenties, small, narrow eyes, beardless, a wide flat nose, frizzy hair. He looked like he had just woken up.

"Who are you?" Officer Hamid asked curtly.

"The building guard." The young man still sounded half asleep.

"What's your name?"

"Abdel-Salam Kahila."

"Where's the owner of this building?"

"He's not here."

Hanash pushed past the young man and entered the foyer. He climbed several stairs and saw a series of mailboxes exactly like those they had just seen in the company. Hanash opened some of them.

"None of them are locked. The office spaces are still unoccupied," the guard explained.

"When's the building owner going to get here?" Hamid asked as he inspected the young man more closely.

"Maybe this evening," he answered indifferently, as he passed his hand through his hair.

"Where are the cartons that these mailboxes came in?" Hanash asked, eying the guard closely.

"The carpenter who works here took them," the young man answered without hesitation.

"Where can we find this carpenter?"

"I don't know. But he'll be here tomorrow."

Kahila shrugged and sighed as though fed up, and added dismissively, "If you want to rent an office space, come back tomorrow when the holiday's over."

He left them standing in the foyer and disappeared down a corridor.

After leaving the building, Hanash and Hamid jerked to a stop simultaneously and exchanged perplexed smiles. After months of not being able to take a step forward due to the lack of information, now that they had seized the beginning of a solid thread, they seemed struck by a kind of paralysis.

It seemed farfetched to think that this empty building could be directly connected with the murderer. Solving the case couldn't be that simple after all those weeks of getting nowhere. They had to find that carpenter who, according to the guard, had taken the empty cartons. They felt it better not to press the young man further on that matter, or to reveal that they were police. There was always the possibility that he'd inform the carpenter, giving him the opportunity to flee or destroy any incriminating evidence. And, of course, they had no concrete proof that the cartons in question came from this particular building. There were other buildings on the company's list that might have purchased mailboxes around the same time. They needed to make inquiries at those buildings as well.

*

Back at the station, Hanash called a meeting in his office. After reading his team in on the latest developments, he instructed them to check out all the buildings that had recently bought the Spanish-made mailbox units, and report back to him with the information they collected—every detail, he stressed, no matter how seemingly trivial. They were not to let on that they were police, he added, and then assigned one officer the task of conducting a background check on the personnel manager at the al-Saada company.

After the men left, he sat back in his swivel chair and closed his eyes. Something was nagging at him. He wasn't comfortable with the way he'd handled that guard at the Manar building. Perhaps he and Hamid had been too cautious, which kept them from asking more questions that might have reaped more details. They should have asked him when he last saw the carpenter take one of those cartons. Why did he take them? How many cartons were there and did he take them all? They should have asked him how well he knew the carpenter, and they could have pressed him for the carpenter's address. Come to think of it, what was to say that the guard wasn't lying when he said the carpenter took the cartons?

He shot out of his chair and strode out of his office, slamming the door behind him. He decided not to let anyone know where he was going. He strode through the corridors without responding to greetings and without peeking into offices, as he usually did, in order to check up on subordinates.

He pulled up in front of the Manar building, got out of his car, and walked through the small garden to the front door. It was locked. He shook the handle, knocked on the glass pane, and rang the bell. He rapped on the glass repeatedly. Taking a couple of steps back, he peered up at the glass façade and shouted, "Is anyone here?"

He went back to the door, bent down, and peeked through the keyhole. No trace of the guard. "What are you looking for?" an angry voice asked, and Hanash spun around. "Where's the building guard?" Hanash asked the man who stood there.

"I haven't seen him today. Maybe he's still asleep."

"I just spoke with him a little while ago. Where'd he get off to?"

"Hell if I know," the man responded curtly.

"Who are you?" Hanash demanded, as he flashed his official ID.

The man shot a hand to his forehead in a military-like salute and assumed a more polite and respectful tone. "I'm the doorman at that building across the street." He pointed to a timeworn apartment building dating from the colonial era.

"Do you know any of the people who've been working at this site?"

"A few of them."

"Do you know the carpenter?"

The man raised his eyebrows and smiled. He was about fifty, in a threadbare uniform. He had a cigarette tucked behind his ear and twiddled another between his fingers.

"There isn't just one carpenter. There's a whole team of carpenters."

"How well do you know the building guard here?"

"Abdel-Salam Kahila . . . I can't say I know him well."

"Does he live here, in the building?"

"Yes. He's got a room."

The middle-aged man put the cigarette between his lips and lit it. He moved passed the detective, rapped on the door, and shouted for Kahila. Still no sound came from within.

"Can you open it?" Hanash asked in a friendly manner.

"I can try."

The doorman seemed glad to be able to perform a service for the police. He extracted a large bundle of keys from his pocket and began to insert them into the keyhole, moving from one key to the next with machine-like rhythm, as though to demonstrate his skill. After several attempts, the door opened. He entered, inviting the detective to follow. He flicked on the lights and shouted, "Abdel-Salam!"

He turned to Hanash and said apologetically, "It looks like he's gone."

Hanash entered a corridor that led to a door at the other end.

"Is this where he lives?" he asked the doorman.

"Yes."

The detective turned the knob. The door opened easily and a foul odor assaulted their noses. The older man flicked on the lights.

"It stinks in here," he grumbled. "This guy's an enemy of hygiene."

Hanash remained silent, frowning as he took in the sparse contents of the small room. There was a narrow mattress, some rumpled sheets, and a filthy quilt. The few clothes were in disarray in a tiny closet with no doors. There was a small dirty table with nothing on it. Everything was visible, hardly requiring an extensive search.

Hanash swiveled in place, allowing his eyes to pan the room, pausing on spots here and there as though in accordance with a preset route. There was something disingenuous about the anarchy in this room, as though it had been searched. Or perhaps the owner had been in a frenzy to find something he'd misplaced—or needed to hide. Hanash's eyes came to a rest on one of the walls. The color looked patchy and uneven, as though it had been hastily repainted. He took his car key and scratched at the paint, which chipped off, exposing dark stains. He touched them with his fingertips, brought his fingers up to his nostrils, and sniffed. Just the thought that these might be spots of dried blood made his skin crawl. He turned toward the doorman, who stood staring, mouth agape. Hanash could see the fear mixed with the astonishment. He clearly sensed the gravity of this situation. Hanash approached the closet and cast a cursory glance at its meager contents, without touching anything. There were only a threadbare shirt, a pair of underwear, a pair of socks, and a black jacket. These are the clothes he left behind, Hanash thought.

He stooped to peer beneath the closet and, right at the back, he found a pair of rubber gloves with what looked like traces of dried blood on them. He exchanged glances with the doorman and said sternly, "Don't touch anything."

The doorman gave a jerky nod. He was unable to utter a word. Hanash lifted a corner of the mattress. There was a school notebook with some pages ripped out. A shiver coursed through his body as he thought of the letter the killer had left between the thighs of his last victim. It was written on the same type of paper as the pages in this notebook. He grabbed his cell phone and barked instructions to have all the members of his team report to the building immediately and to notify forensics to do the same.

As he conducted the guard out of the building, he asked him whether he had Abdel-Salam's phone number. The doorman extracted his cell phone and said proudly, "Here it is, sir."

The detective punched the numbers in on his own phone, only to hear "The number that you are calling is currently not available . . ." He asked the guard whether he had the number of the owner of the building. He did, and gave it to the detective.

Hanash dialed and received an answer this time. He introduced himself formally, asked the proprietor of the Manar building to come to his property immediately, and hung up, cutting off the landlord's inquiries.

He turned back to the doorman and pelted him with questions about Abdel-Salam Kahila. What kind of person was he? Anything unusual about his behavior? What kind of friends did he have? Girlfriends? The man grew wary and protested that he knew nothing. But he summoned the courage to ask the detective the reason for the search. Hanash ignored the question.

9

No one apart from Hanash and the guys from forensics were allowed in the room. Hanash stood guard at the door while the forensics team dusted for prints, examined the paint and stains on the walls, and combed the room for other evidence. The forensic graphologist trained his flashlight on a page in the notebook that Hanash had found beneath the mattress. It contained minuscule impressions of words that matched those in the letter addressed to the police.

"We have some hard evidence here!" Hanash exclaimed triumphantly. "This is the notebook the killer's letter was written in! You can see the letters embossed on one of the pages. You can even make out some of the words. He had pressed too hard with the pen, as you said." He paused suddenly and then murmured, "That means he wrote the letter before tearing the leaf out of the notebook."

He suddenly blanched and felt his stomach knot. The security guard of this building must be the killer. He had just stood face to face with him a couple of hours ago. Images of that young man's face, his pat response about the carpenter taking the cartons, and the abrupt way he disappeared down the corridor flashed though his mind. No, thought Hanash as he wrestled with his self-recriminations, that guy is not deranged or demented. He's an extremely intelligent young man. He would have certainly seen Hanash on TV and recognized him, and he had the presence of mind to remain calm and play the naive and humble building guard. He'd had the ability to make their conversation seem of no concern to him, and hadn't betrayed the slightest degree of discomfort or confusion.

Hanash could have kicked himself. He and Hamid were the butt of that charade. Hanash could still picture the man's face, inches away from his own. The guy had no resemblance to the type of maniac who could have committed all those horrible murders. He seemed like an ordinary kid, no different from other young men his age. Nothing whatsoever in his appearance aroused fear or suspicion.

A crowd of gawkers had begun to collect in front of the building. The police ringed the building in order to keep pedestrians away. A short, obese man in a djellaba pushed his way through the crowd. The skewed Andalusian tarboosh on his head and his quivering jowls added to his clownish appearance. When the police prevented him from passing through the cordon, he thumped himself on his chest and protested loudly, "I own this building. Let me through."

Just then the chief of police's car drew up. The guards rushed forward to clear a passage for him, shoving the landlord aside in the process. They snapped to attention and raised their hands to their foreheads in a military salute.

The landlord shouted, "What's happening in my building? Would somebody please tell me what's going on!"

Hanash greeted Commander Mohammed Alami at the main door of the building. In a voice strained from fatigue he said, "The guy who worked as a security guard at this building . . . he's our man."

"Where is he?" the chief asked, peering around anxiously.

Hanash sighed. "He's cleared out. There's no sign of him here. I've put out an APB."

"You mean he's the one responsible for all those unsolved murders?"

"If not all of them, at least the last one. We have some hard evidence."

A smile appeared on the chief's face. "What led you to him?"

He would have liked to say that he had spent all night at the computer until he cracked the code that put them onto this building. However, sensing that this was not the time to boast, he merely said, "The cartons in which he had packed the remains of the victim."

Once the police chief left, Hanash was unable to think calmly or keep his mind on the work of the forensics teams. He still couldn't believe that he let the killer give him the slip. He'd been hoodwinked, goddamn it! He'd let a doltish-looking doorman with a guileless smile pull a fast one on him. He prayed the news wouldn't get out. The ridicule he'd have to bear!

He stole away from the forensic crews. Grabbing Hamid by his jacket sleeve on the way, he led him out of earshot of the others.

"The perp's the building guard we met earlier," he whispered. He tried to steady himself, then spat out, "We had him in our hands and we let him get away!"

Hamid's eyes widened. He'd been with the teams assigned to check out the other buildings on the al-Saada company's clients list. He stepped back in disbelief. Then he howled with laughter. No one else on the force could laugh so openly in front of their commanding officer. Though in this case it was clear that Hamid's laughter was synonymous with a wail.

"This will stay between the two of us," Hanash said firmly.

Hamid nodded. Mostly to comfort his CO, he said, "Even if we let him get away, we made him do it so quickly that he left us evidence."

At last the landlord was allowed through to speak with Hanash. News that this building was associated with the serial murders and that the doorman was implicated had spread through the crowd of onlookers. That explained the pallor and dazed expression of the landlord, who began to speak before Hanash even had a chance to pose a question.

"Abdel-Salam, my building guard and doorman. . . . Yes, the polite, bashful young man who was always ready to lend a helping hand. . . . He has never shown a bad side or a tendency toward violence. Everyone around here liked him."

The detective greeted this with a smirk. "So, where's he now? Do you know?"

"He must be on some errand. He'll be back soon."

The landlord extracted his phone, dialed his doorman's number, and received the automated out-of-service message. He looked at Hanash with a bewildered expression.

The detective brought his face close to the landlord's and snapped, "Does he have family here in Casablanca?"

The landlord jerked his head back, his eyes widening. He had wanted to stick to the defense of his doorman and clear his building of all suspicion. This affair could ruin sales of office space. But the detective's authoritative tone threw him off balance and made him feel that the glare of suspicion had fallen on him, too. In a trembling voice, he said, "He's got a sister here in Casablanca. She works as a maid in the Oasis quarter."

The detective whipped out his notebook and tiny pen and took down the sister's name. Tearing out the page and handing it to Hamid, he said, "Take Bu'u and Miqla and track her down. Be careful."

Hanash felt certain that the landlord knew very little about his doorman. The rotund little man was merely worried about the reputation of his property and its value in the real estate market. And no wonder. He could hear the murmurs among the gawkers about the shadow of scandal and the evil eye that would haunt the building. Probably, photos of the "ill-fated" Manar building had already begun to circulate across the internet.

"Is the whole building empty?" the detective asked off-handedly, mainly to see how the landlord would respond.

"Yes, it is," the landlord answered, somewhat startled by the question. "It just needs some slight alterations and the final touches in the lobby. We also have to wait for some bureaucratic problems to get sorted before we launch the sales campaign. Hopefully that will be done soon."

"Where did this doorman come from? How did you get to know him?"

"He's from south of Marrakesh. From the village of Ait Ammi, to be precise. A lot of people from that village have migrated to Casablanca. They find jobs as doormen and building guards because of their reputation for honesty and courtesy."

Hanash grinned and shook his head. "Is he married?"

"No. Single. When I gave him the room, I told him that if he wanted to marry, he'd have to quit, because the room wasn't designed to accommodate a whole family."

"Friends and acquaintances?"

The landlord heaved a sigh. About the last thing he could possibly care about was who his doorman's friends were. But to please the detective, he supplied an answer. "He has no acquaintances to my knowledge. He's a shy young man who keeps to himself. . . . Oh, and he's been to university. He has a BA in math."

Just as I suspected, Hanash thought. Our prime suspect is no country bumpkin. He had the intellectual faculties and scientific mindset to create riddles and tricks for the police.

The detective narrowed his eyes at the landlord and asked with a hint of suspicion, "How can you defend him so strongly? He murdered and mutilated his victims, possibly right here in this building. He might be responsible for at least four murders. . . . Have you ever seen any women with him?"

"I have properties and businesses all over town, not just here. I don't know more than what I've already told you."

"What types of places did he frequent?" Hanash pressed.

"How in God's name would I know?" the landlord whined.

Hanash left the crime scene and returned to his office. He was exhausted, but a jumble of thoughts kept racing through his mind. He had to coordinate a manhunt in several directions. He unbuttoned his shirt collar, sank back into his chair, and swiveled it halfway around. He still could not forgive himself for letting Kahila slip through his fingers. He pictured the guy standing there, right in front of him, looking him squarely in the eye without flinching. And no wonder: The suspect was no dimwit. He had a brain—a BA in math, no less. It was impossible to get into that faculty without an excellent academic record. He smiled wistfully as he thought of Tarek. His son just couldn't get his mind around math. He flashed back to the face of that young guard. How could that kid from some remote, desiccated village in the south have committed such atrocious acts? Where did he get such evil impulses?

He swiveled back to face his desk and set to work with a spurt of energy. Snatching up the phone, he dialed a number at the office of the public prosecutor to ascertain that an arrest warrant had been issued for Abdel-Salam Kahila. Then he called Central Records and had them send over a photo of Kahila, taken from his ID card, which he dispatched along with a nationwide APB instructing all checkpoints and security facilities to search and arrest said suspect. Hanash then dialed a number that connected him with the Ait Ammi gendarmerie. After reading them in on the investigation, he warned them that the suspect was extremely dangerous and that they should take the utmost precautions when apprehending him, should he be present in the village. He also asked them to initiate official interrogations of all family members, relatives, and associates.

Hanash was interrupted by a knock on the door. Hamid entered together with a young woman in her early twenties. Her faded djellaba, the kerchief set high on her head and tied behind her neck, the scuffed plastic sandals on her feet, and every feature of her face spoke of the hardships endured by servant girls forced to help out their poor families by working for the well-to-do. The resemblance was striking. Hanash could tell she was Kahila's sister at first glance.

"This is his sister, Zuhra," said Hamid. "She works as a maid with the minister's family."

Hanash opened his desk drawer, pulled out a photocopy of a picture, and showed it to her.

"Do you know this person?"

She blinked and replied, "It's Abdel-Salam . . . my brother."

Hanash heaved forward in his seat. "When was the last time you saw him?"

"On the first day of the feast. He came to the place where I work . . . the home of the family I work for."

"Why?"

"He hardly ever came to visit me. I hadn't seen him for two years, maybe more."

"So why'd he come? What did he have to say?"

"He didn't say anything much. Maybe he came just to wish me a happy feast. But he just stood there at the door. He refused to come in, even though the lady of the house said that he could come in and have lunch with me in the garden."

"How did he seem? Did he seem scared? In a hurry?"

She frowned and hesitated for a moment. Then she said, "He was strange. He seemed tense. He'd open his mouth to say something, then close it again. I asked him if he'd done something wrong at work and gotten fired. He said no."

The detective and officer exchanged a quick glance. Hamid, who stood in front of Hanash's desk facing Zuhra, understood that he was to take over the questioning.

"He didn't tell you where he was going?"

"No. I felt that maybe he was sorry he came to see me."

"What was his relationship with his parents like?"

"Our father died a long time ago."

"And your mother?"

Zuhra moaned softly and seemed on the verge of tears, as though the question had reopened a wound that had never healed.

"Our father had left us a plot of farmland. Our house took up part of it and on the rest we grew vegetables. But when the area was rezoned as urban land instead of agricultural land, the price went up, and this big shot from our village, a parliament member who belongs to the ruling party, came up with some documents to prove that my father had sold him our land while he was still alive. That guy won his suit almost overnight. But my mother refused to carry out the court's ruling. She attacked the MP, got arrested, and was sentenced to a year in prison. She died in there. Afterward, me and Abdel-Salam came here to Casablanca. I found a job as a servant and he got a job as a doorman."

"Didn't you have the deeds to prove that you owned the property?" Hanash asked.

"When my father was still alive, he and that big shot were always fighting over that piece of land. In the end, he exploited my father's death to get what he wanted."

Soon after identifying the prime suspect in the four open homicide files, a surge of apprehension crushed Hanash's newfound zeal. What if Kahila was preparing to strike again? And what if he succeeded despite all the precautions they'd taken? Police forces throughout the country had been put on the alert, more personnel had been assigned to the manhunt, and security had been tightened everywhere. But there were still no leads to his whereabouts. Because of the paucity of available information, Hanash had three of his men go back and interview the doorman of the apartment building across the street from the Manar building again. Previously, the older man had given them the impression that Kahila seemed like a normal guy: shy, not very outgoing, and not the type to cause trouble. But after being pumped by Baba, grilled by Bu'u, and turned over to Kinko for some extra sweating, he changed his story. Kahila used to rent out rooms in the empty premises he was guarding for illicit sex. At least one of the suspect's victims might have been a prostitute.

After the success in identifying the Manar building, Hanash caved to Tarek's demand for a pair of sneakers—an outrageously overpriced brand. From then on, Tarek granted himself the right to interrogate his father about the case and dissect its minutest details. Hanash indulged his son when he could—for example, while he prepared his special chow for Kreet or took the dog for a walk. During one of their late-night strolls in the company of Kreet, Tarek said, "This Kahila file reminds me a lot of American serial-killer movies. The perp in those films always had a troubled childhood and is psychologically disturbed. He kills in order to wreak vengeance against society and he imagines that by doing this he's performing a public service. He's the kind of person who always has problems with women and sex."

Hanash turned to look at his son with a curious mixture of feelings. All the cases he'd worked on before were far more straightforward: a fit of jealousy or burst of rage that ended with a stabbing or a bullet, a theft gone wrong, a dispute that turned violent and spiraled out of control. Yes, there was the occasional deliberately planned act of revenge, but the majority of homicides he'd dealt with were unplanned and the perpetrator would regret his action immediately. Stunned and confused, he might panic, but with nowhere to run or hide, he would often turn himself in or be quickly apprehended. But this case was different. Hanash was more certain than ever that the suspect had been inspired by some American film. Certainly his trail of murders had all the ingredients of a film: a killer who rents out rooms for prostitution, then chooses his victims from his customers, kills them, and brutally mutilates their bodies. Could this be a way of venting anger at possible sexual impotence?

Hanash smiled at his son as he affectionately scratched Kreet behind the ears and shooed the flies away from him. "Right, sir. Now that you're one of the team in this case, what do you propose as our next course of action?"

Tarek returned the smile, and said excitedly, "How about sticking up wanted posters with mugshots of the killer in all public places and broadcasting them on TV and the internet, offering a reward for information leading to his whereabouts?"

"That won't be possible on the public TV stations because the government doesn't want to spread panic. Also, if we put a price on the murderer's head, who's going to pay it? That kind of thing happens only in the movies."

Despite such reservations, Hanash felt that his son's suggestion made sense. Ever since the police had learned the suspect's identity, the press had returned to its staple sources of sensationalism: scandal and the private lives of film stars, singers, and soccer celebrities. The "Butcher of Casablanca" was no longer juicy enough for headlines or even for their rumormongering. He'd have to incite their curiosity again and make them drool for morsels of news.

The first thing he did when he entered his office the following morning was phone up a journalist he knew, now the editor in chief of a high-circulation tabloid that was notorious for its yellow journalism and had a popular online edition. Speaking in a hush and only after a long silence, to suggest that he still had strong doubts about what he was about to say, he said, "I'm speaking on the condition of confidentiality. . . . I'm going to send you the most recent photo of the prime suspect in the serial killings case. Publish it with the caption 'Wanted: Dangerous Killer.' Add whatever embellishments you like. Just publish the picture on the front page. Later, I'll give you the latest scoop in this case."

After hanging up, he went through the same routine with other tabloids.

The following morning, the pictures were splashed across the front pages of the country's newspapers beneath such headlines as "The Butcher of Casablanca: Still at Large."

Kahila's picture went viral on Facebook and other social-networking sites, which warned: "He's still out there! He could be standing right next to you!"

That evening, the officer who had been assigned to keep the Manar building under surveillance knocked on Hanash's office door and entered. He had with him a woman in her twenties wearing a worn djellaba and a kerchief on her head. He held her by the arm as though afraid she'd bolt.

"She came to the building and asked for Abdel-Salam Kahila," he explained. Hanash was both surprised and delighted. He examined the woman closely and broke into a wide smile. He leaned forward, looked at her amiably, and asked gently, "Why did you come to that building asking for Abdel-Salam?"

"I saw his picture in the papers and on Facebook."

Hanash signaled to the officer to leave. Then he got out of his chair, walked around his desk, and took the seat in front of her. Her eyes widened in alarm.

"Who are you, my dear?" he asked, as though talking to his own daughter.

She wavered a moment, then stammered, "I'm . . . my name's Samira Nour. My sister, Nezha, went missing here in Casablanca and I'm afraid she might be one of his victims."

"When was the last time you saw her?"

"I haven't seen her since September last year."

Hanash practically jumped out of his seat. He knew the dates of the murders by heart. September was when they had discovered the first victim.

"And you haven't talked on the phone since then either?"

The young woman looked down at her lap, at a loss, as though expecting to hear bad news.

"Look at me," Hanash said firmly. "Hasn't your sister called you even once since that date?"

"No. . . . I work as a maid for a family in Rabat. I don't have the time to come down to Casablanca to look for her. I'm just a maid, sir."

"What did your sister do?"

Samira bowed her head. Hanash gave her the time to collect her courage. She knitted her eyebrows and sighed. Then she muttered, "She'd go out with—"

Hanash cut her off in order to relieve her embarrassment. "Do you and your sister have family here in Casablanca?"

"Our family's from the village of Baba Mohamed near Fez. But our parents were poor, so they took us out of school and had us work as servant girls in people's homes. I've been working for a family in Rabat since I was ten. My sister worked for a family here in Casablanca. But she was raped by the father of that family and then fired. She was left homeless and eventually she fell into prostitution." She paused to collect herself. "I lost touch with her for several years and then she began to visit me from time to time in Rabat. But not since September last year. I've had no news from her at all since then. Then yesterday, I came across Kahila's picture in the newspaper and read that he murders women. So I came to Casablanca to look for my sister."

"Do you have a picture of her?"

She opened her small handbag, took out a small photo, and handed it to the detective. It showed a rather pretty young woman, seated with her hands in her lap. He contemplated the photo closely, then looked up at Samira. The resemblance was striking.

Hanash hesitated for a moment. With a sympathetic look in his eyes, he said, "It's hard to answer your question. Kahila mutilated his victims' faces to keep us from identifying them. Do you think your sister had a relationship with him?"

"I don't know, sir."

"Leave me your phone number and address. We'll keep in touch with you." Hanash picked up his office phone, punched a number, and barked a command. A moment later, the door opened and an officer walked in. Gesturing toward him, Hanash told Samira, "Right now, I want you to accompany this officer. He's going to take you to a lab so they can take some swabs from you to see if it helps us identify one of our victims. There's no reason to be alarmed. It's a very simple test."

In less than twenty-four hours, tests confirmed the identity of the first victim: Nezha Nour.

It was Dr. Wafa Amrani who achieved the next breakthrough, and scored a personal triumph in the process, when she surprised all with her remarkable expertise in forensic facial reconstruction. Not only had she invited other specialists in this discipline, the forensic investigators and technicians, and the criminal investigation team and other ranking police officials to her presentation at the University Hospital, she also ensured that plenty of representatives of the written and televised press were on hand. She waited until her audience fell silent and all attention was trained on her. Then she whisked away the cloth from a plaster bust of a finely sculpted young man in his late twenties. Some uncontrollable laughs escaped some audience members, even from the section where Hanash and his team were seated. That young man was extraordinarily handsome. It was as though Dr. Amrani had given him the features of a celebrity she fancied instead of a person who'd had the skin flayed from his face and his skull crushed.

"The face is a human being's primary means of communicating with others," Dr. Amrani said. "It expresses our emotions and our thoughts, consciously or unconsciously." She explained the difficulties she had encountered in reconstructing the chin, the lips, and the rest of the features. As though delivering a lecture to a class of her own students, she proceeded to explain in detail why forensic facial reconstruction needed to go beyond the physiological level to the reproduction of a face that people would see as natural and recognizable.

Sadly, there was there no missing-persons file matching this victim's face, which confirmed Hanash's theory that the victim probably belonged to that class of lost souls in Casablanca who had no family or loved ones to search for them.

But no sooner had the reconstructed face of the last victim—digitally enhanced—circulated across the internet than Hanash received numerous phone calls from diverse parts of the country.

They all turned out to be false leads until Hanash's office received a call from Sidi Taibi, a coastal village located about 140 kilometers north of Casablanca. The caller claimed to be the brother of the victim. The precision of the information he provided led Hanash to dispatch Hamid to the village to question the man and verify his information.

"Take Bu'u with you," Hanash said. "I want a full report. Don't leave out a thing. You'd better shine if you want to marry my daughter."

Hamid's eyes lit up with joy at his boss's faith in him: sending him on such an important task solo. He felt a wave of relief, as though Hanash had just given him the green light to date his daughter. He hadn't gone out with her, been invited to their home, or seen her at all since Eid al-Adha. There'd only been a few hasty phone calls with no time for words of affection or intimacy.

Hamid returned with some good news from Sidi Taibi, which is situated in what was once a fertile agricultural area but that had succumbed to a drought that turned its fields into dusty and arid wastelands. "There's a strong resemblance between the man claiming to be the brother and the reconstructed face of the victim," Hamid told his boss.

Once the DNA tests were conducted, there was no longer a shadow of a doubt. The police had now confirmed the identity of the first and fourth victims: Nezha Nour and Abdel-Qader, the brother of a villager in Sidi Taibi. The prime suspect, in these two cases at least, was Abdel-Salam Kahila.

No sooner was he notified of these results than the chief of police invited Hanash and senior officers in CID to a meeting in his office. Hanash, who had brought with him a thick dossier on the homicides linked to the prime suspect, had intended to open the meeting with a strong introduction that he'd round off with congratulations all around. However, just as he was about to speak, he wavered. Despite all the hard work and the good results so far, he shouldn't take too much credit, not when the perpetrator was still at large and could strike again at any moment, and two of the victims remained unidentified.

"In light of the results of the DNA analyses, combined with other information acquired in our investigation, we can presume that the first victim, Nezha Nour, was probably in an illicit relationship with the fourth, Abdel-Qader. As for the second and third victims—one female, the other male— their identities remain unknown. No missing-persons reports have been filed for persons of their age and complexion who disappeared around that time. Nevertheless, we now know that Kahila rented out some rooms in the Manar building for illicit purposes and that at least two of his victims were among his customers.

Commander Alami shot forward in his seat and thrust his index finger into the air: "Remember, this criminal is out there wandering our streets among us. He may come from some rural backwater, but he's an intelligent, educated man and every murder he committed was performed in a manner meant to defy us and prove that he can outwit us."

Bringing the meeting to a close, the chief urged the officers to dedicate their fullest energies to the case. "The whole of Morocco, not just Casablanca, is clamoring for Kahila's capture before he can kill again."

Before Hanash reached his office, his cell phone rang. The caller was the landlord of the Manar building with some garbled story about the contractor, a guy called Mohamed Ali, going missing along with a sizable sum of money that the landlord had given to him to purchase materials. Hanash asked for the contractor's full name, address, and phone number and said he would see what he could do.

Hanash ended the conversation abruptly. He felt a tingle of excitement and didn't want his voice to betray him. That story of the vanishing contractor was significant. First the building's security guard is revealed to be the killer, and now the contractor disappears with a sizable sum. Where could he have gone? And what could this mean?

The initial inquiries produced nothing. The contractor's phone was out of service. He was unmarried, and a search of his apartment yielded no evidence of plans to abscond or even to travel. According to the neighbors, he was an upstanding, kind, and mild-mannered man who had no enemies that they knew of. He had no relatives in Casablanca, they said. He came from Salé, where he had a brother who was married with a family. He was supposed to have spent the feast with his brother's family, but after contacting the brother, Hanash's team discovered he had not shown up in Salé.

He had no record of theft and there was no evidence of personal motives for turning to theft. He wasn't a womanizer. He wasn't an alcoholic or drug addict. There was nothing to suggest he was a victim of blackmail. Moreover, an inquiry at his bank revealed he had considerable savings in his account, which he hadn't touched in over a year.

Hanash began to weary of the questions racing through his mind. He wanted to find a solid thread linking the contractor's disappearance and the murderer. What if this was Kahila's next victim?

Then he had a flash of inspiration. Up to now, he'd thought of the room of the absconded guard as the crime scene. Yet, given that the guard was the only inhabitant of the building, the entire nine-story office block should be considered the crime scene. He snatched up his phone and asked Hamid to report to his office.

"Do you mean we're going to have to search the building again?" Hamid asked after Hanash explained his brainstorm.

Hanash smiled apologetically and said, "Unfortunately, the elevator still doesn't work. But there's no getting around it. The building has to be searched again, top to bottom this time. We'll put all available men on it."

Four vehicles set off for the Manar building. The detective had issued a call for volunteers from members of the force on leave. The landlord was waiting for them in front of the building. He seemed on the verge of tears as he opened the door.

"Why did the press have to mention my building by name? I'll never be able to lease office space here. I'll go bankrupt!" he cried.

"Then change the name," Hanash said.

"There are photos of it all over the internet!"

Hanash looked up at the splendid façade. Now, where could Kahila be hiding? he thought. He didn't go back to his village. He doesn't know anyone here in Casablanca. His sister was probably the last person to see him. The detective refrained from adding that, actually, he may have been the last to see him.

The police began the combing operation, working up from the ground floor. On each landing there were four doors opening onto palatial offices: large reception areas, spacious rooms overlooking the boulevard, elegant conference rooms. The offices weren't furnished yet, but their clean, modern lines were impressive. The men split up into two teams and proceeded rapidly from office to office and floor to floor. The smokers and overweight officers were the first to curse the lack of an elevator as they wheezed and sweated their way upward. They had to finish before sunset because the upper floors of the building weren't completely wired yet.

By the time the teams reached the ninth floor, out of breath and dripping with sweat, they still hadn't found anything. Hamid opened the window in one of the offices and peered out. He took his phone out and rang Hanash, who had returned to the station.

"We're on the ninth floor. The view's fantastic from up here!"

"You haven't found anything?"

"Some cigarette butts here and there. They probably belong to the workers."

"Is that all?"

Before Hamid could answer he heard one of the officers shouting for him. From that horror-filled voice Hamid knew they had discovered something important. Keeping his phone on so that Hanash could listen in, he followed the detective to the top of staircase, where he had discovered a way up to the roof. A foul stench began to assault his nostrils. Then he reeled in horror at the sight before him: shreds of human flesh, parts of a human face, torn and tattered women's clothing, a meat cleaver, a huge glistening knife, a few razor blades, and walls splattered with dried blood. In another room, they found several bottles of a powerful caustic acid and parts of another body, which had not been completely corroded.

DNA tests established that the partially decomposed body parts were those of Mohamed Ali. The assumption was that

Kahila had killed him, too, but hadn't dismembered the body and gotten rid of it like the others.

Kahila's MO had become clearer: He killed his victims in his room, decapitated and dismembered them, and took most of the pieces to the top floor, where he dissolved them in acid. After destroying any identifying features, he disposed of the remaining body parts in garbage dumpsters.

Only the contractor's body had been spared the full treatment. This murder was different. It had been hurried and possibly unplanned. Perhaps the contractor had discovered what Kahila was up to on the roof. Or, maybe, now that he was on the run and needed money, Kahila may have robbed the contractor and then killed him.

And where was Abdel-Salam Kahila?

10

HANASH AND ALL THE MEMBERS of his team were fired up with
an unwavering zeal and energy, now that it looked like the
arrest of Abdel-Salam Kahila was only a matter of time. Also,
it would be very difficult for him to strike again. His face was
everywhere. In fact, some news and media outlets were rak-
ing in fortunes through the sheer inventiveness with which
they wove stories, embellished descriptions, and smeared and
slandered. Some hidden hands had even plastered pictures of
him on dumpsters and garbage bins. Naturally, there was the
concern that he might disguise himself: dye his hair or roam
around in broad daylight dressed as a woman in a niqab. But,
as the days passed, not a trace of a clue or a whisper of a
rumor surfaced as to where he might be hiding. There weren't
even sightings of possible look-alikes.

Another reason why Hanash felt confident that Kahila
wouldn't strike again was that he had no place to indulge in
his passion for mutilating his victims. With his face all over
the place, he would never risk renting a flat or even a room
in a hotel.

Meanwhile, the general state of alert and mobilization helped solve other cases that had gone cold so long ago they'd almost been forgotten. An example was the famous "Sleepers beneath the soil" file, which dated back to before Hanash had been transferred from Tangiers to Casablanca. It was a member of Hanash's army of informants, recruited from the larger armies of street bums, beggars, and itinerant peddlers, who provided the crucial bit of intelligence that cracked the case. He shared a flat with another vagrant who eked out a living by working the coffeehouses and bars, playing the oud. The problem was that he only played one song, a heartrending one by Mohamed Abdel-Wahab that went, "O ye sleepers beneath the soil, I have come to weep." Every night, after completing his circuit, he would head to a desolate place next to the railway line and sing the song one last time beneath a tree. Once in a while, his roommate would accompany him. They'd sit on the ground beneath the tree and crack open a bottle of booze. One night the street bum noticed that his friend strummed his oud and sang with greater passion than usual, eyes welling with tears as they stared at a particular patch of ground. When he finished the song, he went over to that patch and knelt down and kissed it, and then lay on top of it as though making love to it. The bum related the incident to a police officer who was performing one of his routine rounds of Hanash's CIs. It was merely something to report to keep the officer happy; he didn't see anything suspicious in the oud player's behavior. The officer, in turn, relayed the anecdote to Hanash, thinking his CO would appreciate a good laugh. Instead, the story tickled Hanash's sixth sense. He ordered some of his men to go out to that place near the railroad tracks and dig. Much to their surprise, they unearthed the remains of a body. A woman. As would become clear during the subsequent investigations, the itinerant oud player had had a violent falling out with his lover many years before. He'd killed her and buried her on that spot.

Officer Hamid had phoned Manar to give her the exciting news that the case that had been preoccupying the police 24-7 was nearing an end. He invited her out to dinner and offered to drop by her beauty parlor to pick her up after work. She agreed without a second's hesitation.

Hamid paced up and down the sidewalk waiting for Manar to come out and meet him. He saw her assistants leave the beauty parlor one by one. Then, to his surprise, she appeared at the door and signaled for him to come inside. Hamid looked to either side as though unsure she was beckoning to him. He turned back to face her, eyes widened in alarm. What if Hanash dropped by all of a sudden and caught him alone with his daughter? They weren't even engaged yet. Reading his thoughts, Manar reached out and grabbed him by the hand, pulled him inside, and shut the glass door. She asked him to have a seat until she finished getting ready.

Hamid sat perched on the edge of the chair. He felt that there was something odd about her behavior. Suddenly a delicious thrill coursed through him, making him put his police instincts on hold. He peered around the salon, taking in its large mirrors, plush chairs, and stylish decor, and his heart filled with joy. All this belonged to his future wife . . . if his luck held. When Manar emerged from the bathroom, he could not conceal his admiration. She'd changed out of her white smock and was now in an elegant emerald-green dress topped by a jacket tailored perfectly to her petite shoulders. She wore matching shoes with heels high enough to make her at least as tall as he. "Um . . . perhaps we should be going now?" he asked awkwardly. Instead of the answer he'd expected to hear, she looked at him with a twinkle in her eyes and a mysterious smile playing on her lips and asked, after a pause, "So, how do you like my beauty parlor?"

"It's great! May God bless you with success."

She remained standing next to the customers' couch. She was in no rush to leave and seemed to be thinking of a way to prolong the conversation. He was not the type to play naive. He moved toward her, staring deep into her eyes, searching for the answer to a riddle.

"I need to know what you really think. Do you really want to marry a policeman?"

Peering directly into his eyes, she asked, "Do you love me?"

His eyes filled with a profound tenderness. He stepped forward, took hold of her hand, and kissed it deeply. In a voice trembling with emotion, he said, "Love is what makes me want to marry you."

She murmured something indistinct as she felt her head spin and her body go slack. Hamid, holding her by the shoulders, pulled her to him and planted his first real kiss on her lips.

11

CONTRARY TO EXPECTATIONS, CASABLANCA WAS once again shaken by another murder bearing Kahila's signature.

As he drove up, Hanash saw the herd of gawkers held back by the yellow crime-scene tape. They were pushing, shoving, and shouting as rowdily as a horde of football fans. The latest victim had been discovered in one of Casablanca's overpopulated lower-class quarters. Hanash paused before pulling the door handle. He barely had the energy to get out of the car. It was almost nine a.m. The reason the body was discovered so late in the day was that this part of town was not on the rounds of the waste pickers because the pickings in the dumpsters were so poor.

It looked like the same MO again. The body was dismembered and the parts were stuffed into three heavy-duty garbage bags. The bags themselves had no identifying marks. The difference, this time, was in the signs that the perp had been in a rush. Apart from a gash to the forehead, the victim's face wasn't damaged and the bags had not been distributed into different garbage receptacles. Hanash left the moment he learned that forensics would probably be able to identify the victim.

By the time Hanash reached his office the web was ablaze with the latest murder and Kahila's mug stared out of the breaking news bulletins. Hanash rapidly skimmed through the reports on online news sites and flicked through social-networking sites.

Fake news interwove with strange rumors of similar murders in other neighborhoods and alleged sightings of the killer here or there. Hanash felt his stomach growl as he scrolled through headlines like "Kahila Defies the Police!" "Women Still Not Safe!" "He's Threatened to Kill More!" One site posted a map with the GPS coordinates of where the Butcher of Casablanca might strike next.

Work at the station proceeded rapidly. The central fingerprint unit identified the victim in record time. The murderer hadn't taken the time to amputate the fingers. When Hanash brought her up on his computer screen, he saw a beautiful, full-figured woman in her late thirties called Fanida al-Ghali. Married. No children. Unemployed. No criminal record. Despite the different MO, Hanash conceded that it could still be Kahila. If so, he no longer bothered to make his victims unrecognizable. Police had already identified him and his mugshots were everywhere, so they no longer needed to know the identity of his victims in order to identify him.

*

It was around noon when Hanash and Hamid pulled up in front of the victim's home. It was a two-story building located on a side street well away from the main street. Through the iron gate, they could see a small courtyard with well-pruned trees and carefully tended plants. The owners must have annexed the space to the house informally, taking advantage of a bend in the road that concealed the property from the eyes of building inspectors. Hamid ascertained the building number. No sooner did he press the doorbell than a small, wiry old man appeared. He was about seventy, with a pallid complexion, and wore a heavy overcoat over his pajamas in spite of the pleasant weather. Still, he seemed sturdy enough for his age, his posture erect and his eyes sharp. The detective sensed the man was anxious and that he had been expecting a visitor, probably for some time.

His questioning eyes darted back and forth between Hamid and Hanash. Hanash remained silent, fixing his eyes intently on the man while his officer did the formalities. The detective picked up on a tremor in the man's hands, which, combined with the pallor, made him wonder whether he was ill.

Hamid spoke softly so as not to alarm the old man. After introducing the detective and himself, he asked, "May we speak with you inside, please?"

As the man opened the gate to let them in, he asked in a trembling voice, "Do you have news about my wife?"

Neither policeman said a word until they were in the courtyard—a small, well-tended garden, in the center of which stood a garden table shaded by a large umbrella and with several chairs around it. A narrow passageway led to the interior.

"Please have a seat, sir," Hamid said gravely.

The man sat down, his eyes imploring Hanash to speak. Hanash, casting his eyes around the premises, asked, "Who lives here apart from you and your wife?"

"Do you know where my wife is?"

"Can you confirm your wife's name?" asked Hamid.

"Fanida al-Ghali." The man's jaw began to quiver. "I'm afraid something's happened to her. She didn't come to pick me up at the clinic yesterday. She was supposed to meet me after I was discharged. She wasn't here when I got home. I haven't slept a wink all night. Her phone's out of service. Do you have any information about her whereabouts?"

"Could you tell us your name, please, sir?" asked Hamid gently.

"Hajj Belaid Benmoussa."

From his accent they could tell he came from the well-known merchant classes in the east.

Hanash paused for a moment before continuing, then spoke slowly and gently, trying to soften the shock. "Your wife, Fanida . . . may God rest her soul."

"What did you say? Are you saying she's dead?"

Officer Hamid stepped in. "I'm sorry to have to tell you that she was murdered. And in a manner that I find hard to describe to you, sir. . . . We found your wife's body in Rahma.

It had been dismembered and placed into several bags that were deposited in a trash receptacle there. Do you have any idea who might have committed such an atrocious act?"

"How could that happen? Are you sure she's my wife? Do you know what you're saying?"

He looked at Hanash as though entreating him to end the nightmare. The detective felt pity for the man as well as a concern that he might suffer a total breakdown.

"I'm terribly sorry, sir, but that's what happened. When you're ready we'd like you to come with us to the morgue to confirm the identity."

Hamid asked, "Did you or your wife have any enemies? Is there anyone you suspect might have wanted to take revenge against you or against her?"

The man shook his head. He pulled his overcoat more tightly around himself. The blood drained from his face, his body trembled, and he started to slump. Officer Hamid rushed up to support him before he could fall off his chair.

"You have no one else living with you here?" Hanash asked.

Hajj Belaid was unable to speak. Hanash looked at the windows overlooking the courtyard. They were firmly shut. He turned back to the old man, who was still shivering as though running a fever.

At last the old man spoke. "I was afraid something bad had happened, but I'd never expected anything so horrible. I can't believe it."

"Had you noticed any change in her behavior?" asked Hanash. "Did she seem afraid or worried? Had someone threatened her?"

Belaid shook his head and began to mumble to himself incoherently.

"Do you want us to call anyone and have them come over?" Hamid asked urgently, afraid the old man might faint.

Belaid shook his head.

Hanash's phone rang. He was about to ignore it, but he saw the name of the chief of police on screen. He walked to the other side of the courtyard and pressed "answer."

"Yes, sir. . . . It's appalling. . . . A woman. In her thirties. . . . Yes, we've identified her. We're with her husband right now. Similar to Kahila's MO. . . . No, no evidence yet. . . . The investigation has just begun. . . ."

After ending the call, he returned to the garden table, exchanged an anxious and dispirited glance with Hamid, then looked down at Belaid, who appeared even sicker and older as a consequence of the shock. Hanash sat down facing the old man, leaned toward him, and said gently but firmly, "Please try to pull yourself together. We will need some information from you. Do you know or have you heard of someone called Abdel-Salam Kahila?"

Belaid shook his head, his gaze empty.

"You said that Fanida al-Ghali was your wife."

The man nodded as though even that wearied him. Hamid took over the routine questions.

"When did you marry her?"

"Seven years ago."

"Do you have any children?"

"I have children from my first wife."

"How many?"

"Three. My daughter, Fatiha, is divorced and she and her daughter are living with her mother, my first wife. I have two sons. Aziz is married with two sons. He works at the Electricity Authority and lives in Rabat. My younger son, Adel, is a university graduate but he's unemployed."

"When was the last time you saw your wife?"

"I'd been in the Shifa Clinic getting treatment for my prostate ailment. Fanida visited me every day. She'd bring me food I liked and stay with me until the nurses made her leave. Yesterday they discharged me. I waited for her to come pick me up, but she didn't come. I rang her several times, but her phone was always out of service. In the end, I had to go home by myself. I'd hoped to find her there, but there was no sign of her. I stayed up all night. When the call to prayer sounded at dawn, I went to the mosque. After the communal prayers, I stayed on to pray to God to watch over her."

"Did you call anyone to ask after her?"

"I called up her family in Had al-Sawalem village. They told me she hadn't come to see them."

"How about here in Casablanca? Does she have any relatives or friends here?"

"No, sir."

"Didn't you think of calling the police?" asked Hanash.

It was some time before Belaid answered. He seemed so shrunken and remote that for a moment Hanash thought he had fallen asleep. But finally the man looked up and said, as though irritated by the question, "That was what I was going to do when you came."

"What was your relationship like between you and your wife?"

"Excellent. It couldn't have been better."

"What about between her and the family of your first wife?"

"There was no contact between them."

Sensing that his answer had sounded too abrupt, he explained, "When I divorced my first wife and married Fanida, my children thought I'd gone crazy. They did everything they could to have me declared insane and lock me up in an asylum. They weren't really interested in my mental health, of course, let alone my happiness. They wanted my money."

He suddenly began to rock back and forth, wailing. "Who could have done this to you, Fanida? How can I live without you? How am I going to wake up in the morning and not find you by my side?"

He burst into tears, slapped his cheeks, and gave full vent to his grief like a recently bereaved widow. It seemed pointless to continue to question the old man in his current state of anguish, but when he'd calmed down a bit, Hamid persisted and tried to keep Belaid focused. He pressed him a little more about his first wife and her family, but the old man was incapable of answering clearly. Then the inspector tried a different tack.

"Tell me a bit about yourself, please. How did you first meet Fanida?"

The old man heaved a sigh and smiled as he immersed himself in happy reminiscences.

"I met her at the wedding of a daughter of one of my friends in Had al-Sawalem. . . . I'll have you know that I'm quite well off. I own quite a bit of farming land there and the only gas station in town. I also own three buildings here in Casablanca and I have a respectable amount of savings in the bank. All that is thanks to hard work and the grace of God. But my children, damn them all, aren't like me. They take after their mother, who spoiled them rotten from the day they were born. She said I was cruel and miserly and that I kept them in hardship despite my good fortune. She and her rotten children want everything to come to them easily, without having to lift a finger. They hate work. But I wouldn't have cut them off if they hadn't behaved like their mother when I decided to marry Fanida. . . . You know, son, at first I didn't want to divorce the mother of my children. I would have kept her and given her and her children a decent income. I was even ready to turn some of my property over to them. . . . I really don't want to dwell on the past. It means so little to me now. But if we must rake it up, I'll tell you this, son: They bribed a doctor into writing a certificate stating that I'd gone senile and was no longer able to manage my financial affairs. Then they filed a suit to have me institutionalized. Before that, they stole my checkbook, forged my signature, and withdrew a lot of money from my accounts. Fortunately, thanks to my lawyer Sayyid Shukri—he's a member of parliament, I'll have you know, and a partner of mine in some of my businesses—I turned the tables on them and got them off my back. If I'd wanted to I could have had them all sent to jail."

Hamid didn't need all those details, but he hadn't wanted to interrupt the old man.

"Do you have a maid?" he asked.

"Lalla Tamou. We call her when we need her. But Fanida does most of the housework. She's a fanatic about cleanliness and order."

"Are you sure we can't call anyone for you? A member of your family or a friend?"

"I'll call Fanida's parents. But . . . but how will I ever tell them what happened to their daughter?"

When Hamid asked whether he was going to inform his first wife and children, Belaid knitted his eyebrows and looked away. After a pause, he sighed and said, "I haven't spoken with them since the day they wanted to lock me away in the nuthouse. I can't bear to see their faces. . . . Except for Adel. He was still young when they started to plot against me. He's the only one I help out financially, because he studied hard at university and got his licentiate. But he hasn't been able to find work yet. . . . He writes poetry. If he'd studied economics, I'd have helped him start a business."

Simply as a matter of routine, Hanash asked the old man a second time whether he'd ever heard of the serial killer Abdel-Salam Kahila.

"Never heard of him. But what's that guy got to do with my wife?"

The question was left unanswered. Hanash signaled Hamid that it was time to go. He'd begun to develop a dislike for the old gasbag.

After leaving Hajj Belaid's place, there were two tasks that needed doing. First, they had to question the neighbors, visit the old man's family, and find others who may have known the victim and her whereabouts. This he delegated to Hamid and an inspector of his choice. The second task he had to do himself, as it entailed spending the rest of the day in his office and working his way through his list of informers. There had been a long lull since the last homicide. Then suddenly another one occurred bearing the marks of the previous ones. Kahila was the thread they needed to follow. But so far, none of the police's surveillance and tracking systems had managed to get a trace on him. Hanash needed a tip-off in order to move forward.

Rahma, where Fanida's remains were found, was a popular quarter situated miles away from anywhere Kahila had operated so far. In that kind of neighborhood, where everyone knew everyone else, he couldn't have just snatched his victim off the street if he'd had no previous connection with her. And where would he have taken her to murder her and do his grisly butchering work? Where could he be hiding? It would be next to impossible for him to rent an apartment, what with the new laws and regulations put into effect as part of the security precautions against terrorism. He'd need a proper ID, and the landlord would surely have notified authorities of his new tenant immediately. As clever as he might be at disguising himself, he could never alter his appearance entirely. Wanted posters of him were everywhere. Mugshots had been distributed to all neighborhood wardens, who knew the minutest details about everyone in their jurisdiction. These government-appointed officials had their own informants, too. Every doorman, building guard, grocer, and neighborhood resident was willing to furnish them with the latest gossip and tip them off should anything unusual occur. The wardens were also responsible for submitting signed daily reports, which would include information about a newcomer or a significant event. These were entered into the precinct ledgers, given a sequence number, and archived. In more urgent cases, the warden could phone or report in person to his superior. It would be fair to say that word of mouth was the mainstay of the national security services. It was and remains far more effective than surveillance cameras and the latest digital technologies, which are always vulnerable to damage and malfunction. Plus, however sophisticated and precise they may be, they lack the human instincts of suspicion and alarm. In short, there was no way Kahila could rent a place in any corner of the city without security agencies catching wind of it.

Still, there are always unpredictable twists, thought Hanash.

When Hamid knocked and entered his office, Hanash could tell immediately that he had come back empty-handed. He motioned Hamid to a chair, listened to his report, and felt his anger rise. There was not a single useful item apart from the fact that Belaid's former wife could barely hide her delight at Fanida's demise. To be sure, she wailed and cried, but they were obviously crocodile tears.

"They're all packed into that tiny apartment, which reeks of dirty diapers," Hamid recounted, referring to Belaid's grandchild from his divorced daughter.

"What about the unemployed son with a university degree?"

"He wasn't there. His mother told us that she had no idea where he was. He hadn't spent the previous night at his home, but she said that he did that often. I had Baba continue the search for him."

There was a knock on the door. A security guard entered and saluted the detective.

"There's a woman here who wants to speak with you. She said she's Fanida al-Ghali's mother."

Without answering the guard, Hanash got up, strode over to the door, and opened it to invite the woman in. Hanash was immediately struck by the resemblance between her and her daughter. She wore a loose-fitting djellaba and a kerchief riding high on her head and tied at the back of her neck. When she reached the center of the room and stood between Hanash and Hamid, she tried to be the first to speak, but her face grew pale and her lips trembled. However, as Hanash asked her to take a seat he thought she seemed more uncomfortable than distressed, as though she hadn't yet heard the news about her daughtert. Hamid, also unsure whether she had heard about her daughter, struggled to keep the pity out of his face while Hanash kept his voice neutral.

"What can I do for you, ma'am? I'm Detective Hanash."

She hesitated before speaking, as though unsure how to comport herself in front of these two officials.

"Could you please tell us your name first?" asked Hanash, as a way to encourage her to speak.

"Aisha Haddad, Fanida al-Ghali's mother." She reached into her purse to extract her ID.

"That won't be necessary. Please continue," Hanash said.

"Thank you. . . . My son-in-law, Hajj Belaid, phoned me and told me something horrible had happened to my daughter. He said . . . he said you found her dead . . . killed . . . and that her body had been cut up. I came to tell you that the body you found . . . it can't possibly be my daughter."

"Have you seen her this morning?"

"No."

"Has she phoned you?" asked Hamid.

Hanash extracted a photo of the victim that Belaid had provided from his desk and showed it to her.

"Is this her?"

"It's a pretty old picture. But yes, that's my daughter. But she couldn't have been killed."

"Could you tell us why?" asked Hanash.

She shifted her eyes back and forth between the detective and the officer, as though about to confide a secret.

"The day before yesterday, my daughter came to the village to attend the wedding of her best friend. She didn't want to tell her husband, who was still in the hospital. If she had, he wouldn't have given his permission. He's a kind and generous man, but he's the jealous type. . . . My daughter spent that night in the village. Yesterday morning she took the bus back so she could be at the clinic before noon in order to bring him a change of clothes and take him home. . . . Please don't tell him what I just told you. As I said, he's jealous and might start imagining things."

Hanash, who'd been observing her intently as she spoke, asked, "Did your daughter call you after she got back to Casablanca?"

"Yes, she rang me from her home yesterday evening. She said everything was fine, that her husband had been discharged from the clinic and was in good health. But then her husband called me today to tell me that they found her cut-up body in a dumpster. How can that be? She called me up just yesterday evening and sounded perfectly normal. In fact, she was happy to have her husband back home and relieved that the tests showed he didn't have something malignant."

Hanash was uncertain how to proceed. He glanced at Hamid, signaling him to take it from here, and then contemplated the photo in his hand as though searching for inspiration.

The inspector, for his part, struggled to order his thoughts while Aisha waited expectantly for a response, confident that she'd opened the officers' eyes to their grave mistake. The two men were momentarily lost for words.

Then Hanash reached into a drawer, pulled out a picture of Kahila, and presented it to the woman. "Have you ever seen this person before?"

The woman took a quick glance at the picture, wrinkled her nose at the ugly face, and shook her head.

Hanash picked up the phone and dialed the morgue.

"Doctor Wafa Amrani, chief medical examiner."

After some brief pleasantries, he turned to business. "Can you tell me anything about the items that came your way?"

After a moment's pause, Dr. Amrani said, "I haven't started work on them. I can't give you anything yet. I'm sorry."

"I have somebody here who might be able to do an ID. We'd like to have a look right away."

"That's possible. But I can't promise you more information until I begin work on it."

He hung up and glanced over at Aisha to find her staring at him in alarm. She was an attractive woman in her sixties. Although her eyelids had begun to sag and the bloom had gone out of her complexion, her face was unwrinkled. Hanash would have had Hamid escort her to the morgue, but he felt that Dr. Amrani would have refused to break protocol for the younger officer.

The chief medical examiner emerged from the corridor leading to the autopsy theater to greet them. To Hanash's surprise, her white surgical coat was spotless. Even the surgical gloves she wore were immaculately white. She nodded a greeting to Hanash then turned toward Aisha and said, "You must be her mother."

The woman stared back at the doctor, unable to grasp what she had just heard. Hanash was annoyed by the doctor's candor. Fearful that the woman might become hysterical, he hastened to ask, "May we go inside, please?"

The doctor ignored him. Taking hold of Fanida's mother's arm gently, she said compassionately, "Try to be strong. Her face, thank God, hasn't been damaged."

For a layperson, the interior, with its peculiar odors, was eerie. The staff took pains to keep visitors from feeling too disoriented and confused.

The body was covered with a white sheet. The mother's eyes were fixed on it, praying that it was anybody but her daughter. Hanash, who was sandwiched between the two women, was certain the mother would collapse the moment the doctor lifted the sheet. Dr. Amrani looked at the mother sympathetically and said, "Now try to keep a grip on yourself."

As though performing a delicate task, she carefully turned back the sheet to reveal the victim's face. The hair had been gathered into a plastic surgical cap with the rim pulled down low enough on the forehead to conceal the gash on the skull. The doctor folded back the sheet to just below the chin, hiding the place where the head had been severed from the torso.

Without uttering a sound, the mother reached out, in a mechanical motion, toward the edge of the sheet as though to uncover the rest of the body. Hanash quickly pulled her to his side and asked her gently, "Is this your daughter?"

She nodded, her face taut with pain. Hanash felt her body go slack, her head resting on his shoulder. He steered her firmly toward the door as Dr. Amrani hastened to open it. The doctor followed them out to the corridor and gave an exasperated cry. "How many times do I have to tell them to leave at least one chair here. Nobody ever listens!"

She took out her cell phone and made a quick call. Then, taking hold of the mother's hand, she said to Hanash, "Leave her with me."

"There are certain details I'd like to know about the—"

"I'll make sure you get my report today."

Hanash nodded. He cast a quick glance at the mother. She was now leaning her full weight against the doctor's shoulder, her eyes hollow, her face rigid. He understood that it would be of little use to try to question her now.

On the way to his car, Hanash made a quick call to Hamid.

"I want that other son of Hajj Belaid waiting for me in my office when I get back."

He hung up before the officer could reply. He'd been overcome by that fierce surge of aggression he felt whenever he found himself struggling against the tide. He climbed into the passenger seat of the car, slammed the door, and, without looking at the officer behind the wheel, commanded, "Take me to the Shifa Clinic. Do you know where it is?"

"Yes, sir."

They screeched out of the parking lot. They were in a marked vehicle with the blue light flashing on the roof and the siren wailing, but the traffic was too dense for drivers to pull aside. Hanash fidgeted in his seat and fumed. "This is what Casablanca has come to: Casa chocka-blocka!"

"The more they widen the streets, the more congested they get," the driver ventured cautiously.

Hanash ignored him. He was now focused on his cell phone screen, browsing the internet to see how the latest homicide was playing on the online news and social-networking sites. Every now and then he'd emit a sardonic grunt or wry comment as his finger worked the screen, flicking through dozens of video clips featuring Kahila's mugshot with satirical voice-overs. At one point, Hanash could not restrain a loud guffaw. Kahila's face had been projected onto a two-hundred-dirham banknote. The caption read: "If you recognize the man in the picture, deliver this note to the nearest policeman." Despite it being a jibe at the pervasive bribe-taking in the force, Hanash had a good laugh at it.

*

Inspector Hamid and Officer Baba returned to the home of Lalla Hafiza, Hajj Belaid's first wife. This time they found it hard to persuade her to let them in. Her daughter appeared at the door in an agitated state. Her headscarf had come undone and she kept fumbling to readjust it. What happened to her father's wife was none of their concern, she said curtly. "He's the one who abandoned us and sold himself to that belly dancer."

Inspector Baba thrust his jowly face forward and held up a pudgy hand to silence her. There was a reason his friends nicknamed him "the heavy lieutenant."

"We only want to speak with Adel. Hand him over to us and we'll be gone."

Seeing a crowd beginning to assemble outside, Hafiza opened the door and said in a loud voice, "Please come on in. Let's talk inside," thereby signaling to all and sundry that everything was normal.

After she closed the door she said, "There are only women and children here. Adel isn't here. Go ahead and search— even what we're wearing if you have to."

It was a delicate situation. The ex-wife was getting aggressive and the daughter was screaming in a hoarse wail: "He left us in order to marry a girl no older than me. He showered her with his money and forgot that we, his own children, even existed. He hasn't given us a dirham in seven years. If only it was him that was killed. That would have made us happy!"

"Shame on you!" her mother cut in, though more for the sake of propriety than admonition. "He's your father in spite of everything. If it was him who died, I'd wear black. If not out of love, then out of respect because he was the father of my children." Turning to the officers, she continued: "When I married him, he was dirt poor and couldn't even put dinner on the table. All that money he made was thanks to my patience and endurance. He used to say that when he got rich he'd cover me in gold. But the richer he got, the stingier he got."

Hamid cut her off. "Where's Adel?"

"What do you want with Adel?" Hafiza asked as though suddenly aware of the demand.

"We want to ask him a few questions."

The mother and daughter exchanged nervous glances. Their lips tightened and their faces froze into masks at the suspicion that some accusation was looming.

"Questions about what?" the mother asked.

"Where is he?" Baba repeated.

Hamid said, "The last time we were here you said that he didn't spend the night here. Where can we find him?"

Just then the door opened and Adel walked in. He was a thin, melancholy-looking young man, stooped as though carrying the worries of the world on his shoulders. He had the scruffy beard of a young rebel. He flashed a sarcastic smile, jerked his chin derisively at the officers, and said, "I heard you're looking for me."

His mother and sister rushed to him as though to shield him from the police.

"Where did you spend the night yesterday?" asked Baba, narrowing his eyes at the young man.

"On the beach, counting the stars."

Fatiha's baby started crying in the adjacent room, but Fatiha didn't budge.

"Have you heard about what happened to your father's wife?" asked Hamid.

"The whole town's talking about nothing else. The picture of the two-hundred dirham note with the killer's face on it has gone viral on the internet. You still haven't caught him?"

"We'd like to ask you a few questions," Officer Hamid said. "Could you please accompany us to the station?"

The physician who had been supervising Hajj Belaid's treatment had a fleshy face, broad shoulders, and a totally bald head. Unlike most members of the medical profession that Hanash knew, he did not wear prescription glasses. The physician led him to the nearest empty examination room and spoke hurriedly but guardedly, as though reluctant to divulge a professional secret.

"The nurse told me you're the head of criminal investigations. What can I do for you, sir?"

Unaccustomed to this kind of reception, Hanash momentarily lost his train of thought. He said, "I've come because of a patient of yours, Hajj Belaid. Could you tell me when exactly he was discharged from the clinic?"

The physician smiled. "If you want to know *exactly*," he said, with a sarcastic emphasis on the word, "you can ask someone from admin. They're the ones who issued the discharge slip."

"But he can't be discharged without your approval."

"That's true. Fortunately, after a battery of tests, we found the enlargement benign. The last time I examined Hajj Belaid was yesterday at nine in the morning. As for when he left the hospital exactly—whether it was immediately after that or an hour or two later—admin will be able to give it to you down to the split second."

"Thank you," Hanash said and preceded the doctor to the door and into the corridor.

The doctor caught up with him and pointed him in the right direction. When Hanash reached the administration department, he found several nurses gathered around a computer, cackling at something on the screen. He leaned over and saw that it was the YouTube clip he'd seen earlier, with Kahila's face printed on the banknote.

He smiled and said, "Which one of you was in charge of Hajj Belaid?"

The youngest stepped forward and looked at him anxiously. "Hajj Belaid left the clinic yesterday. Are you one of his relatives?"

"Did he leave by himself, or did someone come to accompany him?"

"His wife came to collect him. Are you a member of the family?"

"What time did he leave exactly?"

"At noon. Who are you, sir?"

Hanash turned abruptly, dismissing the nurse's question with a flick of the wrist, and strode angrily toward the exit.

Why did the old man say that she hadn't come to pick him up yesterday? He certainly didn't have Alzheimer's. Was he so naive that he didn't realize how easy it would be to corroborate his statements?

When Hanash returned to the car, he instructed the driver to take him back to the university hospital, and fast. He snatched his cell phone out of his pocket and rang Dr. Amrani to ask if Aisha Haddad was still there. She responded that she'd had her kept overnight for observation. Thanking her, he hung up, looked down at his lap, and seethed.

Hanash found Aisha in a private room in which she sat at the edge of a bed, ashen-faced, tears streaming from swollen, pain-filled eyes that seemed to stare at the unerasable vision of her daughter on the autopsy table.

With no prelude, he said almost gruffly, "Could you tell me what time, exactly, you called your daughter and she spoke with you on the phone?"

She nodded in the direction of her purse.

Hanash went over to the side table, picked up the purse, and handed it to her. She pulled out her cell phone, flicked through the caller list, and said in a weary voice, "Yesterday in the late afternoon she was at home and alive. I called her at exactly five past five p.m."

*

Hanash entered his office, hung up his jacket, and walked to the window. Sliding the curtain aside with a listless sweep of his hand, he stood staring blankly at the street below. He seemed to have lost every last drop of zeal for his job.

He turned around at the knock on the door. Hamid entered holding Adel by the arm. Hanash smirked. The young man's clothes irritated him more than anything else: baggy trousers with multicolored stripes, a black felt jacket, and a thinly twisted bandanna around his neck.

"Where were you yesterday?" Hanash asked without bothering with introductions.

"I just roamed the streets until I got tired. Then I hung out in the train station coffeehouse until dawn. I do this a lot when I can't sleep."

"What do you have to say about what happened to your father's wife?" Hanash asked, glowering, eyes pinned on his subject.

"We were all wrong about her. We should have tried to remain neutral. There were things we couldn't understand at the time."

"You can leave now," Hanash told Adel.

Hamid looked at his boss, stunned.

After Adel left, Hanash said, "The old man lied when he told us his wife didn't come to pick him up when he was discharged. The nurse there confirmed it. Fanida was at home, alive and kicking, in the company of her husband yesterday in the late afternoon. She spoke with her mother by phone at exactly five past five p.m."

The officer gaped. "Do you mean the old man did it?"

"He can't be so demented that he forgot that his wife took him home from the clinic and that she was with him at five p.m. yesterday evening. Her mother's phone log proves that."

"The damned liar. But could he have even done a Kahila? I mean, could he have even been able to use his methods? And then don't forget he said he'd never heard of Kahila before."

Hanash sighed. "If only Kahila had done it. At least he might have left us some clue that could lead us to him."

He saw Kahila elude his grip again. It seemed less and less likely he was implicated in this homicide. Despite the questions that remained, Hanash felt sure it fell into the copycat category. Kahila had become an inspiration to all sorts of human beasts and domestic savages.

"What can I do for you?" asked Hajj Belaid as he closed the front gate. He turned to find the two men walking toward the front door. He stopped in the middle of the courtyard, but they kept moving until they entered the house. He followed them reluctantly. Inside, Hanash circled the old man then turned to confront him.

"You lied to me, Hajj. Your wife was with you when you left the clinic."

The old man smirked. "Whoever told you such a thing?"

"I checked at the clinic."

"Maybe I forgot," the old man said.

He cast around feebly as though searching for a place to sit. Hamid moved to block him.

Hanash continued: "Why did you lie to me?"

The old man spoke as though nothing mattered any more. "It's over and done with. Fanida's dead. May God rest her soul. They say she married me for my money, but it's not true. People say a lot of things. She was a humble woman. She never asked for anything unless I offered it to her first. I had seven good years with her. She was like a fresh blossom that bloomed for me every day. She gave my life a new meaning . . . made me enjoy the simplest things. Whenever I prayed I'd thank God for blessing me with Fanida."

He began to teeter, so Hamid helped him to a seat. Irritably, the old man fumbled through his pockets. He fished out his cell phone and handed it to the detective without raising his eyes.

"Take a look at WhatsApp. You'll see a video that I received the night before I left the clinic."

As Hanash intently scrolled the screen, Belaid continued, "And all the while, I'm lying there dreaming of her."

Hamid positioned himself next to his boss so he could see the screen as well. Fanida was dancing with amazing skill in the middle of a wedding tent decorated with colored lights. She was in a gown that hugged her body and had a scarf wrapped around her hips, halfway up her protruding buttocks, to accentuate their movements. Her hair was loose and flowing down her back. She winked at someone off-screen. That person soon appeared and began dancing with her, his body almost touching hers . . .

Everything fell into place. Hanash now understood why Fanida's mother had arrived so quickly with the certitude that her daughter could not have been the victim.

"Did she go there behind your back?" asked Hanash.

"Why don't you ask me about that man dancing with her? He'd probably been her lover the whole time she was married to me."

"You told me you'd never heard of Abdel-Salam Kahila, yet you imitated him."

Belaid smiled mischievously and began to speak easily, as though unfazed by his own deeds.

"She's the one who told me about his murders, God bless her. She followed all the news about him. She was afraid to come home late at night in case he'd pounce on her in the street. She was horrified by the news reports about him, but she kept pestering me with all the rumors and jokes. I wish she were alive so she could get a good laugh at his picture on the banknotes." He chuckled, as though all this had nothing to do with him.

"Did anyone help you dismember the body and carry it to the dumpster?" Hamid asked.

"May the Lord have mercy on her soul. She made it all so easy for me. I asked her to run me a bath. I'd already sharpened the cleaver we use for the sacrifice at Eid. In the bathroom, she was bent over the tub cleaning it. I brought the cleaver down on the back of her skull. She toppled into the tub and her blood flowed straight down the drain. The rest was a breeze. After putting her into the garbage bags, I put them into the trunk of my car and drove over to the Rahma neighborhood."

12

WHY DO PEOPLE PREFER RUMOR to fact? The police had released
an official statement announcing that they had solved the last
homicide. They broadcast it over every conceivable media
and furnished the press with details about the identity of the
murderer and his motives. But still, Kahila remained Morocco's digital hero number one, so his images refused to fade
from the networking sites. It would not be an exaggeration to
suggest that he had fans, some so loyal they dismissed the official account and held that the police were merely "covering
up" for the serial killer by attributing his crimes to others in
order to reassure the good citizens of Casablanca.

The phenomenon made Hanash's gall rise. It flew in the
face of truth and kept him from savoring the taste of victory from the last case they had solved. Kahila's insidious
mug kept peering out at him from all corners of the web,
taunting him, reminding him that his work was incomplete
and robbing him of the pride his superiors should take in
his achievement. In fact, security authorities had the Central Bureau of Judicial Investigations (BCJI)—the Moroccan

FBI—assemble an elite undercover manhunt team and tasked it with apprehending the notorious murderer. The BCJI and its covert team were given the broadest powers in order to enable them to carry out their assignment. The accomplishments of this bureau, which was equipped with state-of-the-art technologies, enjoyed extensive coverage in the official media. The media portrayed its operatives— highly skilled agents rigorously trained in fighting terrorists and organized crime rings—like the heroes in a sci-fi film, with their assault rifles, helmets, and those masks that make it impossible to learn their real identities.

It was the day before the first weekend after he'd broken the Belaid case, and Hanash was so discouraged that he had an overwhelming urge to get plastered, even though he hadn't had a drink in ages.

"What are your plans for the weekend?" he asked Officer Hamid in a neutral way so as not to reveal what he had in mind.

Filling his voice with the resentment he felt toward the higher-ups for their ingratitude to Hanash and his department, Hamid answered, "Staying home, sir."

Speaking brusquely in order to hide his awkwardness, Hanash said, "I might drop by your place tonight,"

"Why, sir?" asked Hamid, suddenly filled with trepidation.

"I thought we could crack open a bottle. I'm on edge and I want to take my mind off things a bit. But I don't want to go to a public place."

Hamid smiled brightly. "I'll be expecting you, then." Hamid sent up a prayer of gratitude that Manar's father hadn't decided to drop in by surprise like he sometimes used to do in the past.

Of course, Hanash hadn't missed the officer's sudden alarm. He knew that Hamid had been seeing his daughter in his apartment, which didn't bother him since the two were as good as engaged. Preparations for the ceremony were almost done, lacking only a convenient date.

The officer didn't have to spend a dirham from his own pocket. He merely had to phone up his bar-owner friends and have them send over their finest vintages. Simply being asked for such a favor meant a lot to them. The same applied to the famous restaurant from which he ordered an assortment of appetizers.

When he opened the door for Hanash later that evening, his eyebrows shot up to see his boss in sneakers, a jogging outfit, and a cap with the bill pulled down to hide his face, like a thief on the prowl. His eyes widened further when his boss reached into his sweat suit jacket and pulled out a bottle of high-end whiskey.

The detective swept his eyes around the apartment, an enigmatic smile playing on his lips. Though small, it was beautiful and very close to Hanash's villa.

There was a momentary silence as the two men exchanged glances as though they were at a crime scene. Hamid quickly poured out a couple of drinks and handed one to his boss.

Hanash examined the liquid, then held up his glass toward Hamid's and said, "Cheers." Hamid told Hanash that he no longer drank except on weekends and holidays. "I gave my word of honor to Manar that I'd stick to this rule until I give up drink entirely."

Hanash asked playfully, "You're not going to break that rule even when you get promoted to detective?"

"If that happens, I swear by God that I'll pay for the drinks out of my own pocket!"

The two men laughed. The officer got up, went to the kitchen, and fetched a tray on which he had laid the appetizers. As they worked their way through the drinks, Hanash went over to stretch out on the couch. Hamid hastened to place a small pillow under his head.

Avoiding eye contact with his officer, Hanash said, "We shouldn't pay attention to those rumors. They're totally groundless. We're good at our jobs. We break cases in record time. The higher-ups are just ungrateful."

"They're only interested in catching Kahila to save their own faces. They know nothing about our work."

Hanash shifted his head on the pillow in order to face Hamid.

"He's probably left town. He might even have migrated to Europe on one of those human trafficking boats. Or maybe he signed up with some terrorist organization. But the mercenary press insists on attributing the last homicide to him, even though the real perp's been caught and locked away."

"And that's what's keeping us from getting credit."

The officer poured out a couple more drinks and handed one to the detective, who sat up with some difficulty to accept it.

"I can bet on this," said Hanash as he raised his glass. "If Kahila's still in Casablanca, I swear I'll get to him before anyone else."

He took a swig and leaned back into the couch. Hamid settled back in his seat and stared off into the distance. Hesitantly, due to the diffidence he felt toward his CO, he said, "I'm really glad to be part of your family, sir."

"Let's keep this visit between the two of us," Hanash said. "I don't want anyone to think I'm encouraging you to drink when that was the reason I was initially reluctant to let you marry my daughter."

"I may have been a heavy drinker in the past, sir, but now I only imbibe on weekends and that's solely for restorative purposes after a long week's work."

"Ha! That's a good one! What do you mean by 'restorative'?"

"For alcoholics, drink is a leisure activity. People such as ourselves merely drink as a form of R&R to relieve ourselves of work-related stress. . . ."

Hanash grinned and scoffed, "You sound like a professor."

Hanash saw a helmeted man in a mask like those worn by the BCJI reach into the closet where he hid his gun. He tried to shout, but no sound came out. His body felt numb and immobilized. He jerked awake in a cold sweat, chest heaving, throat as parched as if he'd spent a week in the desert. He was feeling the effects of the night before. While gulping down a glass of water, he remembered that his officer had accompanied him to his house. Then, instead of turning in, Hanash had fetched Kreet and the two of them had taken the dog for a long walk down to the beach, where they'd remained until after midnight, chatting about this and that.

In the morning, Hanash headed to the restaurant of an old friend of his, Rubio, located in Ain Diab. Drinking black coffee after a sumptuous breakfast, Hanash and Rubio exchanged jokes and chatted about the latest political news: the forthcoming elections, the transportation crisis. Rubio owned a hotel that catered to foreign tourists, two elegant cafés, the modern restaurant they were in, and other real estate. Over the years, he and Hanash had forged a solid friendship. Rubio was one of the few people who knew the details of Hanash's unsavory past from his Tangiers days, and vice versa.

But the fact was that Hanash had changed since his scrape with death when he was shot point-blank in his office by Officer Qazdabo. He'd become a sentimental homebody who preferred domestic tranquility to late-night carousing.

Rubio asked his friend how the case of the famous killer was going. Hanash brushed the question aside with a hasty "Nothing new." He didn't even want to talk about his success with his latest file, the homicide perpetrated by Hajj Belaid inspired by the "famous killer."

After leaving his friend, Hanash walked along the corniche. "The 'famous killer' instead of the 'famous Hanash' who's on the case," he muttered in self-derision. The "case of the famous killer"—those words had hit him like a punch below the belt when Rubio said them.

Where had he disappeared to? Once again, his mind dragged him back to how Kahila had fooled him, hiding behind the mask of a naive doorman. He'd fooled Hamid as well. If only one of them had taken a step or two after Kahila when he disappeared down the corridor when they first interviewed him, they might have caught a whiff of something to arouse their suspicions.

Hanash pictured Kahila's small room and its meager contents: a saggy mattress, a small stained and filthy table, a doorless closet with some pitiful rags inside. The windowless room was as dark and dank as a cellar, and putrid. How could Kahila have even breathed in such a fetid hole? How could he have slept? That vile form of entertainment he'd invented for himself—dismembering bodies—was perfectly suited to this den, which he lived in even after converting it into a slaughterhouse. The walls retained traces of blood despite the layer of paint he applied after every murder. After disposing of the trunk and the limbs outside, he took the victim's head and hands up to the top floor in order to dissolve them in acid. That was how he concealed the identity of his victims. . . . Prostitutes were murdered all the time. Hanash suspected Kahila would have had earlier victims—before he graduated to this cat-and-mouse game he was playing with the police. How many victims had he really claimed?

The traffic noises broke into Hanash's thoughts as he walked down the corniche in Ain Diab. Most of the cars speeding by were upmarket models: flashy sports cars, luxury coupés, capacious SUVs. This was an upscale neighborhood with elegant restaurants and cafés, trendy nightclubs and bars, and sophisticated shopping centers boasting the top international brand names. Newspapers abounded with stories about bonanzas, opportunities for making a quick profit, and the rise of new class of millionaires who made their fortunes through bribery, corruption, and the rentier economy. At the same time, crime experienced a boom, making it possible for the likes of Kahila to exist. As Hanash walked, he contemplated the skyscrapers, and the cranes and bulldozers on building sites from which new skyscrapers would rise. The city was a magnet that attracted laborers from distant rural villages. Most of those newcomers had probably been agricultural workers before they packed themselves off to work in fields of concrete as construction workers or, like Kahila, as building guards and doormen, forced to live like rats in the trenches of building sites or in clammy holes beneath the stairwells of apartment blocks. Casablanca had undergone major transformations. But so had crime in the city—so much so that it too sported international "brand names." Casablanca now had its Kahila the Butcher, just as London had its Jack the Ripper.

Hanash jerked his head up to find that he was right in front of the Manar office block. The place was shrouded in silence. What distinguished Sundays in Casablanca, like many major cities around the world, was the reduction in traffic, car horns, and sirens.

The front door was securely bolted. He stepped back and peered up at the windows overlooking the street. There were now five signs affixed next to the door—all engineering and accounting services. Kahila, of course, was the reason why the building was still mostly empty. Had this not been the scene of his homicides, there would have been a high demand for office spaces in this prime location and they would have been worth a fortune. The only option the landlord had was to wait until people forgot the bad omen that plagued the building and that was likely to continue to plague it as long as Kahila remained at large. He was so closely associated with the place that people frequently called it the "Kahila building."

"Hey Chief . . . Commander . . . sir . . ."

Hanash finally realized that someone had been calling him. He focused his attention and found himself staring at a man standing in front of him, hand to forehead in a make-shift salute. It was the new doorman of the building, whom Hanash or one of his officers had been checking in with.

The doorman had opened the door even before Hanash asked to be let in. As Hanash stood in the foyer, he felt a numbness come over him as Kahila's face loomed before him again and he felt his throat constrict at the thought of that nauseating putrid odor from his room. He took a deep breath and asked the doorman, "Any news?"

"All's well, sir. Nothing to report, sir."

Staring directly into the eyes of the doorman, Hanash asked, "Do you live in the same room as he did?" He nodded toward the end of the dark corridor.

"Yes sir. As long as I'm still single." He smiled, and added, "And I'd have to stay that way for the rest of my life if I wanted to remain here."

Hanash smiled back and asked, "Do you mind if I take a quick look at the room?"

"Do you mean . . . ?" The doorman pointed in the direction of his room, surprised and somewhat alarmed at the request.

In fact, Hanash was nearly as surprised as the doorman that he had made this request, which had slipped out of his mouth as spontaneously as his feet had led him back to the scene of the crime. The doorman invited him into the room, where Hanash found that everything had changed. It had been restored to life and was now as clean and tidy as a room in a modest but decent hotel.

When Hanash reemerged from the building and resumed his walk, his mind became absorbed in other questions as he reviewed each chapter of the case and reexamined them through the lenses of different hypotheses. The mystery of Kahila's whereabouts was a constant concern. Kahila had to be somewhere in this city, unless he'd been murdered himself, or had somehow managed to escape overseas. If he'd tried to go to Tangiers to take one of the so-called death boats to Europe, he would almost certainly have been apprehended at a roadblock or by some other security detail along the way.

The possibility of being smuggled onto a boat from the Port of Casablanca was equally remote. It was virtually impossible to enter the Port of Casablanca without a special permit or unless you were an official employee there. Surveillance was extremely tight and covered the whole environs of the port, which was surrounded by high, unscalable barbed-wire walls. In addition to the hundreds of security cameras, an elite team of guards with trained dogs patrolled the area around the clock. The chief reason for such precautions was precisely in order to prevent illegal migrants from sneaking into the port and onto ships bound for Europe.

The strident ring of his cell phone made his heart sink even before he looked at the screen. Who the hell would call him on a Sunday morning if not to tell him bad news? He pressed "answer" and put the phone to his ear. It was the supervising inspector from Central Telecommunications, sounding as though he were delivering a formal communiqué. "Good morning, Detective. Dispatch received a communication from the Fallah neighborhood. A body was discovered in a trash receptacle—"

Hanash cut him off. "Call BCJI. They're the ones in charge of these cases now."

"I'm sorry, sir. But they're the ones who told me to call you. The body belongs to a child."

The victim was on the ground next to a trash bin, covered by a piece of clothing. Hanash lifted the fabric to find the body of a five-year-old boy, thankfully without a mark on his body. There were no signs of violence, amputations, or disfigurement, and he was fully dressed. The only other members of the force on hand were Inspector Hamid, a security guard, and two techs from forensics.

Some meters away, a woman was reeling on her knees, slapping her cheeks, raising her arms skyward, and pitching herself forward to the ground. She tried to fling herself toward the little body, but a neighborhood woman restrained her while another sprinkled water on her from a bottle.

Hanash surveyed the scene. All the doors and windows were shut. A cluster of filthy trash bins stood in the center of the dusty square. Some distance away, he saw a single store open. Looking up, he caught sight of a few heads peering down from the rooftops. Though it was a Sunday morning, a crowd was gradually beginning to collect.

Hamid came over and greeted his boss.

"Where are Baba and Miqla?" Hanash asked, without returning the smile.

"Miqla's en route. He's late because he was on an assignment."

"And Baba?"

Hamid paused, then said, "When I called he told me he was in El Jadida."

"He's not on leave."

As though covering for Baba, the officer muttered, "A close relative of his wife died, so he took her there."

Hanash dismissed the excuse with an impatient flick of the wrist and turned toward the wailing woman.

"That's the mother?"

"Yes. She lives over there," Hamid said, pointing to a building about a hundred meters away.

"Where's the father?"

"We haven't inquired yet."

"Who called in the homicide?"

Hamid nodded toward the open store. "The grocer. He told me that on his way to open his shop at six, as he does every morning, his attention was caught by a bunch of cats circling around something and pawing at it. When he took a closer look, he noticed what looked like hair on a small human head. He said that last night everyone in the neighborhood had joined the search for the child Saad who'd gone missing. No one found a trace of him. The grocer recognized Saad and rushed off to tell the boy's mother and phone the police."

"Has his mother seen him yet?" Hanash asked.

"Yes. The grocer said that after he told her, he and the neighborhood women tried to stop her, but she wrenched herself free and ran over and looked."

"Have the women take her inside so that you can question her."

A forensics technician approached, muttered a greeting, and gave a despondent shrug. "The body's intact. It bears no marks of violence or abuse. The probable cause of death is suffocation."

Hanash's phone rang. He took it out, saw who the caller was, and sighed. It was the assistant chief of police.

"Good morning, sir. We're on-site. . . . Yes, a child of five or six—"

"Well then," the official cut in, "if that's the case then the incident is unrelated to the Kahila file. He's never killed a child before."

"I'll keep you posted as soon as we have more facts."

"Good luck," the security official said and hung up.

Hanash headed to his car and drove off, letting Hamid oversee operations at the scene.

Hamid, heartened by what for his boss was warm encouragement, took a deep breath and headed to the victim's mother's house. The door was open. The front room was a pandemonium of wailing and screaming and people who were all speaking at once. Several women were huddled around the mother, trying to comfort and console her. Her face was gray, sapped of every last drop of energy. He ordered the women to wait outside so he could talk with her alone. As they left, he cast his eyes around the room. On one wall he saw a picture of the child dressed in a circumcision-celebration costume. He looked down at his mother who, he guessed, was in her mid-twenties. Her eyes were bloodshot from crying, her body hunched. When Hamid introduced himself, she reached toward him beseechingly and cried, "Tell me it's not my son!" Then her arm went limp and her body trembled. "My baby!"

Hamid waited until her crying paused and said, "Could you tell me your name, please, ma'am."

"Sumaya . . . Sumaya Mahjoub."

"My condolences, ma'am. Where's his father?"

"He's on his way. He should be here at any moment."

"What's his name?"

"Khaled Wazzani."

"Where does he work?"

"At the port. He's on the night shift this week."

"When was the last time you saw your son?"

"Yesterday afternoon. He was playing with other neighborhood children out front. I was right here. I could hear the Awlad Sidi Rahal troupe arrive and start to perform their music in the square. Saad came in and asked me for a dirham so that he could give it to the troupe. I gave it to him and . . . and . . ."

Seeing her falter, Hamid cut in. "And you didn't see him after that?"

"No, sir." She heaved a sigh to gather strength. "When I went out to look for him, some neighbors who'd been to the Awlad Sidi Rahal show told me that crazy woman, Farida, had come up and asked him where his father was and when he'd return. They said she kissed him and told him that she should have been his mother, not me. . . . I've tried time and again to keep her away from my son so she wouldn't harm him."

"Who is this Farida?" asked Hamid.

"She wanted to marry my husband, but he preferred me over her. She accuses me of stealing him from her. She's set her mind on destroying my home and family. She was always cooing at Saad and telling him he should have been her son."

"Would she go so far as to do this?"

"Who else would do this do my little boy?" Sumaya said with a strangled cry.

Hamid swung around at a commotion outside and the sound of approaching footsteps. Khaled burst into the room followed by Miqla, who was trying to calm him down. Tall, in his thirties, he had a carefully trimmed beard that went well with his high forehead and receding hairline. It was obvious that he'd heard the news. All color had drained from his face. He rushed over to his wife, who cried, "Khaled!" and threw herself into his arms, wailing, "She killed him, Khaled! She killed him!"

The husband joined his wife's tears. The two clung to each other, so immersed in their grief that they seemed to have forgotten the presence of others. Eventually, Khaled worked himself free from his wife's arms. In a reproachful tone, without looking at the others, he asked, "What did you tell these people?"

"I told them about Farida. She kept threatening us and spying on us. It's got to be her who killed him and left his body out front."

Hamid explained, "He was found by the trash can."

Khaled turned to Hamid and said, as though offering an apology, "I don't think Farida is capable of doing anything like this."

"Such matters will become clear in the course of our investigations," Hamid said. "Where does this Farida live?"

"Across the street. Number thirteen."

Hamid gave Miqla a prearranged signal and the two of them left without a word.

After they left, the couple began to quarrel. Khaled lashed out at his wife for her negligence. "You spend all your time gossiping with the neighbor women, jabbering on for hours about nothing!" he shouted. Sumaya froze at this onslaught, gaping as though she'd been hit by a bullet. "I don't need this right now! You should be consoling me and helping me!" she wailed.

Khaled burst into tears. He tried to take her into his arms again, but she turned her back to him and began to sob convulsively. Then she collapsed to the floor.

Hanash agreed with his superiors that it was unlikely that this homicide was related to the Kahila file. This was a crime of vengeance. If you wanted to inflict the cruelest damage on an adversary, you destroyed the thing your adversary cherished the most: their child, in this case. This type of incident was hardly unprecedented among neighbors living cheek by jowl. Hanash recalled a recent one. It had occurred outside his jurisdiction, so he hadn't worked on it. A woman had a fierce quarrel with a neighbor of hers. But instead of avenging herself directly against the other woman, she coaxed the neighbor woman's son into her home, gave him a drink laced with a lethal substance, and deposited the child's body in the neighborhood dumpster. The apparent MO in the current case nearly matched: revenge taken against a third party.

Since Farida refused to accompany the police voluntarily, Hamid had her cuffed and forcibly escorted to the police vehicle. At the station, she continued to thrash and tug at her restraints, screaming, "I'll only speak to the officer in charge!"

"I am the officer in charge!" bellowed Hamid, barely able to restrain himself from slapping her, because no amount of threats or reassurances had worked to calm her down.

At that moment, Hanash opened the door and walked in. Farida leaped to her feet and cried, "They hit me and slapped me!" She held out her handcuffed hands.

Pretending to come to her defense, Hanash barked at his officers, "Take the cuffs off!"

"It was so she wouldn't hurt herself, sir," said Hamid as he signaled to the officer to remove the handcuffs.

Hanash courteously took hold of Farida's elbow and escorted her back to the chair, saying, "Please have a seat, ma'am." The detective could feel the woman's vibrancy. She was young and beautiful, even in an ordinary housedress and without makeup. "If you don't mind, I'm going to ask you some questions."

"What do you want to ask me? You're attacking me. I have nothing to do with what happened to Saad."

"What was the nature of your relationship with the boy's father?"

Hamid silently positioned himself behind her, outside her field of vision. She felt his presence and scowled, but proceeded to answer the question.

"We grew up in the same neighborhood. We played together as kids. Khaled and I were in the same class in elementary school until we dropped out. When he found a job at the port."

"Where?" Hanash broke in.

"At the port," she responded apprehensively, feeling she had let something dangerous slip.

Hanash narrowed his eyes at Hamid as though reproaching him for concealing an important piece of intelligence.

Hamid hastened to explain: "He works at the port. He operates one of those cranes for loading and unloading container ships. He was on shift this week."

Hanash signaled to Farida to continue. Farida's words poured out in a torrent.

"Then Sumaya came along and ruined our relationship. She used magic charms and cunning. She spread scandalous rumors about me. She told everyone that every boy in the neighborhood had had his way with me—really nasty things like that. Before long, Khaled turned against me and fell for her. I heard he got her pregnant before they were married."

"How did you react to that?" cut in Hamid.

She answered without looking in his direction: "I cried until all my tears were used up. The problem is that the whole neighborhood knew he and I were together before he fell for another woman. That affected my reputation, so nobody's asked me to marry them."

Hanash said, in a flat, detached voice, "That's an admission that you have a strong motive for revenge."

Farida could not suppress an enigmatic smile. "Against him or his wife, maybe. But not a child as beautiful as an angel."

Hamid was about to speak again, but Hanash motioned him to remain silent. Farida appeared calm and rational. As though addressing a topic of general interest, he said, "What happened to that child is true revenge. His death will ruin the lives of his parents forever."

She didn't answer, and seemed grief-stricken. Fighting back a sob, she said, "Yesterday afternoon, I saw him following the Awlad Sidi Rahal troupe after they finished their performance. I kissed and hugged him and told him not to leave the neighborhood. He was very dear to me despite how much I hated his parents." Tears began to spill from her eyes. "I saw in him the child I would have had if I'd married Khaled."

"Who do you live with?" asked Hanash.

"With my family—my father and mother, my sister Fatma, and my brothers Idris and Mohamed."

"How did you spend yesterday evening?"

"At home," she said, surprised at his question.

"With your family?"

"Yes. I was with my whole family and our upstairs neighbors. We'd all gathered in our living room to watch the *Talent Hunt* program."

Hanash let out a sigh of despair. They'd check her alibi. "You can go now, ma'am. Do not leave town, and remain contactable at all times."

As Farida stood up, she said, "You dragged me here without giving me time to fetch my purse. I don't even have bus fare with me."

Hamid reached into his pocket and handed her a twenty-dirham note.

"Here, take a taxi instead of a bus," he said coldly.

She flashed him a spiteful smile, "You know where to find me to get your money back."

Khaled hadn't had a wink of sleep. He'd worked the crane the whole night so the freighter could sail at dawn. It was just before midnight when his wife called to tell him that their son had disappeared and that she was out of her mind with worry. At that time he was up there in that glass cabin at the top of the container crane, already in a rotten mood.

His eyes were sunken and rimmed with dark rings, his face was pale, and he found it difficult to raise his voice. He was furious with Sumaya for that outburst in front of the police about Farida, and his rebuke inflamed her jealousy.

"Why are you defending her?" his wife cried tearfully. "Have you fallen for her again?"

"How can you even say that! We haven't even buried our child yet. I don't want you going around accusing her of this."

He fell silent as though troubled by another, hidden, disaster. When he spoke again, it was as though he were trying to convince himself. "I . . . I think I know who might have done it."

His wife gasped. "Who? Who do you suspect?"

"I'm not sure. . . . It's horrible. . . . I'm going to tell you something, but we've got to keep this between the two of us."

Sumaya stared at him, chest heaving. After an unbearable silence, he said, "Promise me that you'll never breathe a word about this to anyone. This has to remain a secret between the two of us, at least until I make sure."

"Tell me! You're driving me crazy!" she shouted. Suddenly, her mouth twisted into a strange smile. "It's them, isn't it?" she whispered. "It's those migrants you snuck into the port, right?"

He nodded, his shoulders slumped in grief and remorse. "I'll learn the truth my own way. If it's them, I'll wipe them off the face of the earth, one after the other."

The mixture of grief, fear, and remorse reunited the couple. Sumaya stepped toward Khaled and took hold of his hand with trembling fingers.

"Tell me what happened. Don't hide anything from me. I'm your wife. Did they threaten you because you didn't give them their money back? Is this how they took revenge against you? So quickly? In this horrible way?"

"How was I supposed to pay them back?" he cried hoarsely. "Where was I going to get two hundred thousand dirhams? My share was only thirty thousand, and that we spent on Saad's circumcision celebration."

"When was the last time you saw them?" Sumaya asked breathlessly.

"Two of them have left the port and have been hounding me every day, trying to get their money back. Every time, we end up shouting and swearing at each other. Recently they threatened me. There's still one guy there, in the container I've been hiding them in. He's afraid that if he left the port, he wouldn't be able to get back in."

"Why didn't you tell any of this to the police when they were here?"

"Tell them what?" he shouted, tears streaming down his cheeks. "Tell them that I sneak illegal migrants into the port and help smuggle them abroad in cahoots with a bunch of crewmen and guards? They'd arrest me on the spot. I wouldn't even have the chance to bury my son."

"You should have asked the migrants to give you some time so you could come up with a solution."

"There is no solution! It's not my fault the operation fell through after I'd already paid the others. Recently, security has been really tight and they transferred the guards I'd struck an agreement with. . . . Besides, where would I get the money even if they gave me more time? Then there's the problem that they're also in debt. They borrowed a fortune to migrate because they were sure they'd be able to pay it back once they settled down and got work in Europe. Now they're being threatened by the people they borrowed from. They all think I conned them."

Sumaya threw herself onto the bed and collapsed into tears. Without turning toward her husband, she asked, "What are we going to tell the police?"

"I'm going to see the one who's still in the port," Khaled said angrily as he strode to the door and left.

The remaining migrant had fashioned a comfortable bed out of cardboard and fitted out the container to make it look like a livable habitat instead of a tomb.

They were standing at the door of the container. "Where are the others?" demanded Khaled.

"Hell if I know," the migrant answered, cool and defiant. "Casablanca's not my town."

Khaled put on a calm front. Suddenly he gave the migrant a violent shove, whipped out the jack handle he'd brought from the car, and smashed it against the migrant's head. Blood oozed out of the gash. Spotting a length of rusty electric cable lying nearby, he grabbed it and used it to bind the migrant. Then he kicked him and roared with an intense rage, "Who kidnapped my son? Who killed him?"

The migrant, stunned and bewildered, squirmed away and cried, "It wasn't me! I don't know what happened to your son. I didn't even know you had a son!"

Khaled shoved him in the face with the sole of his shoe and growled, "The three of you struck a vengeance pact and murdered my son."

The migrant, face streaked with blood and dirt, tried to push himself back to a sitting position. "Let's sort this out rationally."

"Even if you didn't take part in the killing, you know who did it. Give me their names and I'll untie you."

"Are you crazy? I didn't know what happened to your son. And how could I have killed him and gotten back in here?"

"I said, give me names or I'll kill you instead!"

Khaled was crazed. He hadn't slept, and after a night of hard and wearying work, he'd come home to the news that his son had been killed. From deep inside him there surged an overwhelming lust for violence. He laid into the migrant, knocking him back to the ground and kicking him fiercely.

"This is just for starters," he said, chest heaving. "When I get back here, you'd better tell me how I can find the other two. If you don't, I'll keep you locked up here in this container until you starve to death. Then I'll come and fetch your body and dump it in the ocean, where it will rot and nobody will ever recognize it."

By the time he reached home, Khaled was so physically and emotionally drained that his head was spinning and he could barely see straight. Sumaya was leafing through a photo album and weeping. When she saw him come in, she wailed, "Where have you been?"

He didn't have the strength to speak. He threw himself down on the couch and closed his eyes. She bolted toward the couch and shook him violently. "Our life is over, Khaled!" She threw herself at him and started to slap and beat him, crying, "If you know who did this to our son, don't hide it from me and go tell the police the truth. Then let God's will be done."

He pushed her off him and sat up. "The police? What good are the police going to do us?"

Sumaya's eyes widened in astonishment. "Was it the migrants?"

Faced with Khaled's silence, she began to hit him again. He blocked her blows without pushing her away.

"Stop it! Stop it! You spend the whole day gossiping with the neighborhood women, leaving the child out there in the street with no one to look after him. If you'd looked after him like a normal mother, he wouldn't have been abducted right in front of our house. Where were you?"

Sumaya's arms went slack and her shoulders slumped. "Go ahead and blame me. But it was me who always warned you not to have anything to do with those migrants. Now our baby boy's paid the price."

She pictured Saad in front of her: his soft tears when he cried, the innocent peals of laughter when she tickled him. As she continued to recite her son's charms in an anguished voice,

Khaled felt his mind go blank. His face was sallow; his eyes were glazed. He stood up and staggered into the bedroom, threw himself onto the bed, and fell into a sleep as black as a coma.

When Hanash summoned Khaled to his office, his intention was to glean some new information about the port, not to level a charge. Khaled showed up very late for the appointment. His jacket was wrinkled, his jeans stained and saggy, as if the person inside had shrunk. As Hanash invited him to sit, he studied Khaled's face: puffy complexion, eyelids red and swollen, fatigued as though he hadn't slept for days. But what aroused Hanash's curiosity was that he seemed more afraid than sad.

Striking a sympathetic tone, Hanash said, "In situations such as this, when a child's involved, believe me, we're going to find out who did it."

"I hope so, sir," Khaled muttered, avoiding Hanash's gaze. He looked much more uncomfortable than the interview warranted, Hanash thought. Keeping his voice calm and reassuring, he asked, "Do you have any other enemies apart from Farida?"

Khaled shook his head, staring down at his lap. Hanash began to think it almost pointless to ask the questions he had in mind about the port to a person who seemed elsewhere and barely able to express himself. Nevertheless, he persisted: "Do you suspect anyone who might be capable of such an act? Is there anyone apart from Farida who might want to take revenge against you or your wife?"

"No, sir. I don't have any enemies."

Hanash decided to try another tack. "At the port . . . What's your job there, exactly?"

"I work a container crane."

Hanash was looking for some information about any possible illegal migration activities at the port that the police might not know about or that might even involve some police on the take. In particular, he wanted to learn if there were any way Kahila could have infiltrated the security barriers or been smuggled into the port and onto a ship as part of some human trafficking scheme. There was no other avenue of escape from the city without him having to surface and risk being recognized. Hanash continued to contemplate Khaled in silence. He sensed that Khaled wanted the interview to end, as though he were no longer desperate to learn who killed his son or as though he were afraid that if he talked too much he'd let something slip. Yes, thought Hanash, he's hiding something.

This time, to Hanash's surprise, the medical examiner called him before he called her.

"Who would do this to an innocent child? This makes me regret ever choosing forensics as a career. This is . . . this is heinous."

"Sometimes I regret choosing this profession, too," Hanash replied. "If I could start all over again, I'd become a college professor who gets a three-month holiday so I could spend my time in the pursuit of knowledge."

After a brief silence, Dr. Amrani sighed and said, "It's the parents' fault. How could they be so negligent? How could they leave their children outside, totally unsupervised, until something like this happens? Have you formed an idea about the perpetrator?"

"We've formed an idea about a perpetratress," he replied sarcastically. He was beginning to enjoy this conversation.

"A woman?"

"What was the approximate time of death?"

"Between midnight and three a.m. at the outside. I've only just begun the autopsy, but the cause of death is definitely asphyxiation."

"No sexual abuse?"

"The body is completely unscathed. You'll find all the details in my report."

He could hear another mournful sigh before she hung up. She was strongly affected by this case. It betrayed a certain weakness, despite her outward appearance of strength. It's maternal instinct, thought Hanash as he settled back in his plush leather chair and stretched until his joints cracked.

There came a knock on the door. It opened and in heaved the corpulent Officer Baba, face flushed.

"Welcome back," sneered Hanash.

"I'm sorry, sir. I was wrong. I shouldn't have left without official leave. But it was an emergency. . . . It had to do with my brother-in-law passing away."

"This makes the third time you've killed your brother-in-law."

Baba stuttered. A deep scarlet infused his dark complexion. Hanash felt a surge of pity for the obese officer whose eyes were hidden behind glasses with lenses as thick as the bottom of a beer bottle. He was diligent and thoroughly dedicated, yet he hadn't received a promotion for twenty years.

"As long as you did it, you should have called me up before you returned and told me that you were in El Jadida. Then I would have looked the other way."

Baba bowed his head, and his shoulders slumped.

"You may leave."

13

HANASH INSTRUCTED HAMID TO DRIVE him to the home of the parents of the murdered child. Hamid felt stung. He'd had the impression that he was handling the case.

"Have I done something wrong, sir?"

"Not at all," Hanash answered. "It's just that I've got a hunch about Khaled. He's hiding something. I'm not sure what it is but I want to get to the bottom of it."

While the detective had apparently eliminated Farida as a suspect, Hamid was determined to defend his point of view. "True, Farida has a good alibi. But there still remains the possibility that she hired a contract killer."

Hanash, focused on his cell phone screen, responded, "It's a remote possibility at best. Even if the idea occurred to her, where would she get the money to pay for one? Plus, I'm not convinced she's the sort of person who would do that."

After a brief silence, he scoffed, "The media is deaf and dumb on this murder. At most, poor Saad gets a line or two along with a picture of a kid from some foreign film."

"It must be from the shock that the homicide didn't have Kahila's MO written on it."

"Copy that," said Hanash as they pulled up in front of Khaled's and Sumaya's house.

Sumaya opened the door after the first knock and looked at the men with hollow, dark-rimmed eyes. "Have you found the person who killed my child?"

Hanash adopted a comforting tone: "Rest assured, we'll have him in custody soon. Is your husband in?"

She paused, then mumbled something unintelligible. Noticing how his question had flustered her, the detective asked her to raise her voice. "Please speak up, ma'am, so I can hear you. Is your husband in?"

Her eyes widened in alarm at the tone of Hanash's voice. "He went to the port," she said reluctantly, after which she bowed her head and fell silent.

She's hiding something, too, thought Hanash.

Sumaya mumbled an excuse and turned to go inside as though the interview had ended. Hanash stepped in after her with a determination that took Hamid by surprise. She turned around, contemplated them silently, and heaved a sigh as she battled conflicting thoughts. She took a step back, casting about for something to lean on.

As though to help her out of her predicament, Hanash said, "Your neighbor, Farida, had nothing to do with what happened to your child, did she?"

He noticed the muscles in her jaw work as she tried to formulate her response. Before she could change her mind and the opportunity slipped out of reach, he asked, "Do you suspect someone else? If you have anything to say, don't hold back. We're speaking about your son. I can't imagine you'd hold his life so cheaply as to allow the killer to go free."

Something seemed to click in the woman's mind. With an almost imperceptible nod, she looked directly into Hanash's eyes and said, "My son's blood is dearer to me than anything else in this world. . . . . My husband suspects the migrants."

To help the woman over the last hurdle, Hanash said, "Your husband was helping migrants sneak into the port, wasn't he? Why would he suspect them of killing your son?"

"A smuggling operation fell through. They wanted their money back and they were threatening him."

"When did your husband leave for the port?"

"About a quarter of an hour ago."

Hanash wondered what might have made Khaled head off to the port if it wasn't urgent. He told Hamid to step on it and power up the siren to max. They reached the port in twenty minutes. The guard at the gate saluted as their car drew up and screeched to halt.

"Where's Khaled Wazzani?" Hanash called out urgently.

The guard glanced down at his logbook and said, "Usually he works with the ships that dock at Pier Four."

"How did he get here?"

"In his private vehicle, sir."

"Vehicle model and color?"

"A white Fiat Palio."

The port was like another city. It had wide streets, circular intersections, and street signs pointing to the huge warehouses, cold-storage facilities, and the many piers that jutted like teeth into the dark waters of the Atlantic. Hamid was forced to turn back and retrace his route several times before eventually finding Pier Four, which turned out to be empty—not a single ship was docked there. They returned to the closest traffic circle and asked a port employee if he'd seen a white Fiat Palio. "Yes, it headed that way," the man said, pointing toward a mountain range of unused shipping containers at the far end of the port.

It was another world. Discarded shipping containers stacked on top of each other formed long lanes and filthy alleyways. Some containers appeared to have been tossed here and there haphazardly, their doors torn off and rusting. The lanes between the containers were at most two meters wide, barely enough for their car to pass. After several turns in which they failed to locate Khaled's car, they were forced to get out of their vehicle and complete the search on foot, their hands covering their noses to filter out the penetrating stench. Some containers had been put to use as animal cages. Others seemed to serve as caches for wires and copper parts that had probably been stolen from machines. At one corner, they saw an alleyway that had been given a makeshift canopy of corrugated iron. The Fiat Palio was parked to one side. They approached silently, and then spotted Khaled. Hanash reached for his gun.

Khaled caught sight of them and froze. Then, as though unfazed by their presence, he disappeared into a container. They hurried after him and jerked to a stop at the sight of the migrant slumped against the container wall, his hands bound and his head hanging down on his chest. He was dead.

Officer Hamid snatched the flashlight from Khaled's hand. He bent down, lifted the migrant's head, shone the flashlight on the face, and turned to the detective with a stunned expression.

In a strange, hollow-sounding voice, Hanash said, "Open those doors all the way and get some light in here."

Hanash shone the flashlight in his face again and removed all doubt. It was Abdel-Salam Kahila.

"You didn't recognize him?" Hamid asked Khaled in disbelief.

Khaled, in a stunned daze, shrugged and said, "He was just another migrant. The others left. He got to like this place."

"You've never seen his picture before?"

"No. Why? Is he some sort of celebrity?" His tone was caustic. He'd lost hope in everything.

The officer pulled out his phone, called headquarters, and issued the necessary instructions. Eyeing Khaled suspiciously, Hanash shot out, "Did he admit to killing your son?"

Khaled stood motionless. Hanash shook his head. He tried in vain to keep the pity out of his voice. "You killed him without obtaining a confession. Not only did you kill our ability to learn the facts about many murder cases, you also hampered our task of finding whoever murdered your son."

"I didn't mean to kill him, sir," Khaled blurted out, as though finally aware of his horrible deed.

Hanash pointed to the gash on Kahila's head and the dried blood on his clothes.

"You didn't do that?"

"I didn't mean to kill him."

"This person," said Hamid, "was the object of a nation-wide manhunt. If you had identified him and reported him to the police, you would have been a national hero instead of ending up a killer yourself."

Back at the station, Khaled spilled his confession. He used to conceal one or two migrants under the seat of his van when one of the guards who was in on the game was on duty. Then he'd assemble them all into one of those large freight containers that are stacked on an unused wharf designated for disposables. The migrants had to stay hidden there for anywhere from a few days to several weeks until the arrangements to smuggle them aboard a boat were ready.

Khaled, in his statement, acknowledged that others gained from the operation. From the money he took, he had to pay off the guards, the crew members, and others in the ring. He also had to pay for the food and drink to keep the migrants alive until they left.

The last operation would have gone as smoothly as the previous ones had it not been for an unexpected malfunction in the ship that had been arranged for them. Although the migrants had been notified of the delay, they were so eager to leave that they left the container before the new departure time, almost blowing the lid off the operation and imperiling the ship workers. So the ringleaders called off the deal. Not only was Khaled to unable to recoup the money he'd spent; as the intermediary he became the victim of an amount of malice he could never have imagined. He tried his best to reason and bargain with them, but to no avail. They threatened to take revenge if he didn't return their money or make new arrangements for them. Eventually they left the port—apart from Kahila, who seemed to have taken a liking to the place but, as he now knew, was actually using it to hide from the police.

There was no evidence that Kahila was implicated in the Saad file, which remained open. The fate of Khaled, now in custody, was tragic. If Kahila had murdered his son, at least Khaled would not have committed murder for nothing.

The morning after they discovered Kahila, Hanash received a curious phone call from the chief medical examiner, who told him that the murdered child was a "zouhari."

"Are you telling me that Saad might have been murdered by treasure hunters?" Hanash asked.

"That's exactly what I'm saying," she said.

Like everyone else in headquarters, Hanash knew that Officer Baba was a zouhari, and had heard the story about how Baba, as a child, had been abducted by treasure-hunting 'wise men,' known as fiqis. "Well, then," said the astonished Hanash to Hamid after ending the call with Dr. Amrani, "Let's see what Baba has to say about this."

He issued the order to have Baba report to his office pronto, and before long the officer appeared at the door, panting, and snapped to an exaggerated salute.

"At ease," Hanash said with a smile. "You're not in trouble. Take a seat."

Hamid offered the chubby inspector an encouraging smile. Baba, still trying to catch his breath, plunked himself down on a chair. He sat rigidly and wordless, waiting for Hanash to address him.

"You're a zouhari, right?"

Baba perked up. He raised his hand, fingers up, palm forward, and extended it toward the detective. "As you can see, this line goes straight across the whole palm. It's the path to treasure. It's why I was abducted when I was five years old. By a stroke of luck, my uncle caught sight of me with my kidnapper at the bus station. When he called out my name, the kidnapper tried to escape. But my uncle managed to catch up to him and hold him until the police came. The abductor confessed that he'd been watching me for days. When he ascertained I was a zouhari, he took advantage of a time when no one was looking to kidnap me."

"Tell me exactly what or who is a zouhari," Hanash said as he settled back into his plush seat.

Baba launched into an explanation with enthusiasm. "A zouhari could be someone who has a line going straight across their palm, like I have. Or they might have one eye looking in a different direction from the other. Or they might have a straight line going the length of their tongue. Treasure hunters believe that zouharis are the offspring of jinn and that the jinn snatch human babies from their parents the moment they're born and replace them with zouharis. The human parents believe that they're raising their own child, whereas in fact they're raising jinn children. This is why wise men believe zouharis are endowed with the gift to see things human beings don't."

Hamid burst out laughing. Hanash contemplated Baba. "So, you're a jinn, Baba," he said.

Baba blushed and said, "I don't believe such superstitions."

"Kidnappings of zouhari children are very common, especially in lower-class quarters. The medical examiner has learned that Saad, the murdered child, was a zouhari. Maybe that's why he was abducted and killed."

"It's impossible that the parents hadn't realized he was a zouhari. You'd think they'd have taken the necessary precautions to protect him from treasure hunters."

"That we can easily find out," said Hanash, thoroughly intrigued. "The question is why the kidnappers would return him dead, leaving his body in a dumpster in the middle of the square."

"They believe that they are supposed to kill the zouhari after finishing with him, regardless of whether or not his supposed gifts led them to their dreamed-of treasure. The child would not be returned to his parents alive."

Hanash leaned forward and spoke in a grave tone. "Very well then, Baba. As long as you're a jinn, I'm going to assign you the task of following the zouhari thread of this investigation. The other thread is the search for the two migrants who'd been in the shipping container with Kahila—the ones Saad's parents think are responsible. I think we'll proceed in these two directions in tandem unless evidence emerges to point us elsewhere."

Hanash put Hamid in charge of the search for the other two migrants. Baba started to stand up to leave, but Hanash motioned him to remain seated. Smiling, Hanash said, "Now you're my CO in this zouhari trail."

"Even in jest, I couldn't pretend to be your superior officer, sir."

"So long as we're pursuing this zouhari path, I am at your command."

"In that case, sir, let's go."

Baba didn't utter a word during the whole trip to the Fallah neighborhood. He was at the wheel, but he was not a skillful driver. He'd take shortcuts that turned out to be "longcuts" because the streets were too narrow to allow them to pass the cars in front of them. To break the tedium, Hanash asked, "Have you ever been part of an investigation of this sort?"

Baba shook his head without turning to look at Hanash. At last they pulled up in front of Khaled's and Sumaya's house and knocked on the door.

"Don't let my being under your command embarrass you," Hanash said, his voice calm and friendly. "You're the jinn here. No matter how high my rank is in the force, I'll never reach your level in the jinn world."

Baba stared at Hanash, at a loss for how to respond.

Evidently no one was at home. Sumaya must be out and they knew that Khaled was in custody awaiting prosecution on the charges of manslaughter, human trafficking, and unlawful restraint.

"I wonder where the wife is."

"With her son murdered and her husband in jail, the best place to go would be a mental institution," said Baba with a grave face.

Hanash smiled and raised a skeptical eyebrow.

Baba said, "As long as I'm leading this investigation, sir, I propose a brief recon of the neighborhood."

Baba preceded Hanash into the grocer's, the one who had discovered the body. By the way Baba circled the grocer with a train of routine questions that seemed to lead nowhere, Hanash began to suspect that the officer was up to something. All of sudden, Baba told the grocer, "You're from Souss."

Responding in the dialect of the Amazigh from the Souss region, the grocer said, "Yes, sir, I'm from the village of Imintanoute."

Baba took off his thick, fogged-up glasses, wiped the lenses on his jacket with agonizing slowness, and replaced the glasses on his nose. He studied the grocer carefully, then said, "I bet you knew that the murdered child, Saad, was a zouhari."

The grocer mumbled something indistinct. The silence built as he fumbled with some objects on the counter while working out what to say. To Hanash this was enough to arouse suspicion. He paid closer attention to the interview without interfering.

"I've got nothing to do with such nonsense," the grocer said as he turned to arrange some biscuit packets on the shelves.

"I bet Saad used to buy candy from you. When he held out the money, you'd have seen the palm of his hand, wouldn't you? You're from Souss. The wise men from Souss are the only ones who know how to read the zouharis' palms, aren't they? They're the only ones who can tell how those lines lead to treasure."

"I'm not a wise man, sir."

"Maybe you're not a wise man. But I bet you know a wise man back home."

Baba's tone was sharp and accusing. As he stepped further inside, he added, "Little Saad was killed because he was a zouhari. You're from Souss. Who do you think did it? You must have a theory."

"I can't understand what makes you make think a poor grocer like me would have anything to do with this," the grocer said heatedly. He was a short man with a round, pale face and piercing eyes. His most curious feature was his disproportionately small hands.

"If I were a wise man involved in treasure hunting you wouldn't find me here, living alone, hundreds of miles away from my family, in this cave in the middle of this filthy neighborhood with nothing but garbage for a view."

The detective was impressed by how coolly Baba responded to this.

"I haven't accused you of murdering the child. But I think you know something. So you're going to accompany us to the police station where we can spend some time discussing things calmly."

"Discussing what things?"

"Things like zouharis and treasure hunters."

"I can't help you with those things. I'm just a grocer."

"You're a grocer from Souss. And we have a homicide victim who was a zouhari child."

The grocer was forced to lock up his shop and leave.

Hanash took the wheel this time. He was enjoying playing the role of obedient aide. When he glanced up at the rearview mirror and caught sight of the grocer in the back seat, it struck him that the man no longer resembled a humble grocer.

At the station, the man was taken to Baba's office for preliminary questioning. It was a cramped, windowless office with two desks and no visitor's chair. The grocer grew still and somber as he entered this alien setting. Baba asked for his ID and passed it to Hanash, who'd positioned himself in a corner where he could observe the proceedings in silence. Baba unleashed a battery of questions with the general purpose of

233

wearing the suspect down. Where was he on the day Saad was killed? When was the last time the child came into his shop? How well did the grocer know the child's parents? Baba then turned to the grocer's family in the village: names and occupations of his parents, siblings, cousins, and uncles. Eventually the grocer confessed that one of his uncles in Souss was a wise man. Baba suddenly thrust the palm of his hand into the grocer's face and narrowed his eyes at the man.

"You see? I'm a zouhari, too. When I was a child, I was abducted by a man from Souss. He might even have been from your village. He was a wise man who specialized in treasure hunting. But I was lucky. I was saved by pure chance."

At this point, Hanash stepped out of his corner, placed a hand on the grocer's shoulder, and said in an amicable tone, "You'd better answer the officer's questions. Don't spoil his mood and make him angry."

On cue, Baba slammed his fist down on the desk and shouted, "He's already spoiled my mood. I am angry!"

He removed his jacket and rolled up his sleeves with a menacing slowness.

"Time's up for the legal niceties. I asked him simple questions and got no answers."

The grocer's eyes widened in alarm. He was certain the two men were about to torture him. He stared openmouthed at Baba and then began to speak.

"The child wouldn't stop crying. I put my hand over his mouth to make him shut up, but he suffocated."

"Where did this happen? In your store?"

The grocer burst into tears. Hanash gently put his hand on the man's shoulders again and said, as though to console him, "It is what God has willed for you. It's your fate."

"When did you bring him into the store?" Baba yelled at him.

The grocer's voice filled with bitterness and remorse. "That afternoon when the Awlad Sidi Rahal troupe performed in the square. I took advantage of all the noise and commotion. While everyone was watching the troupe, I lured the child into my store. I'd known he was a zouhari ever since he was a baby. When I told that to my uncle, the wise man back in the village, he came here to check out the child for himself. That was about a month ago. We agreed that I'd kidnap him. Then, after we'd extracted the secret of the treasure and divvied it up, I'd planned to return him to his family, somehow . . ." His tears started to flow again. "But he just wouldn't stop crying and screaming after I'd trapped him in the store . . . and he suffocated to death."

Hanash filled in the rest. "Then, that night, you put his body next to the dumpster and in the morning you pretended to discover him."

The grocer nodded mournfully. But Baba exploded with pent-up fury: "No child abducted by one of your charlatan wise men has ever been returned to his family alive! Once the zouhari leads them to the so-called treasure, they have to bargain with the jinn guarding it. They are meant to use the child's blood as a bargaining chip! After I was abducted I had a miserable childhood. I grew up frightened, closely guarded by my parents, and I was never allowed to play with other children."

Despite the successful close of the tragic case of Saad Wazzani, it was the discovery of Abdel-Salam Kahila that dominated the news. The chief of police convened an official press conference, inviting newspaper representatives from across the political spectrum. Authorities broadcast the news about Kahila across all media platforms, presenting it as a victory that crowned the indefatigable efforts and selfless sacrifices of the country's law-enforcement agencies in the course of their unswerving dedication to the security and safety of the people. Heads of these various agencies took turns fielding hundreds of questions.

Hanash kept his remarks brief and general. He didn't have a flair for eloquent sound bites, and anyway, he was not entirely satisfied. It was coincidence, not a carefully planned and executed operation, that led to the capture of Kahila. He summed up the whole affair with the well-known Moroccan saying: "A grand funeral procession for a dead rat." After having terrified the largest city in the country and confounded the police for months, Kahila ended up killed while cowering in a squalid rathole. To Hanash, the case ended there. He had no desire to talk about it.

SELECTED HOOPOE TITLES

Bled Dry
by Abdelilah Hamdouchi, translated by Benjamin Smith

Whitefly
by Abdelilah Hamdouchi, translated by Jonathan Smolin

The Final Bet
by Abdelilah Hamdouchi, translated by Jonathan Smolin

hoopoe is an imprint for engaged, open-minded readers hungry for outstanding fiction that challenges headlines, re-imagines histories, and celebrates original storytelling. Through elegant paperback and digital editions, **hoopoe** champions bold, contemporary writers from across the Middle East alongside some of the finest, groundbreaking authors of earlier generations.

At hoopoefiction.com, curious and adventurous readers from around the world will find new writing, interviews, and criticism from our authors, translators, and editors.